'We both want a baby.

We both want to be loving parents, committed to the baby, but not to each other. And that's why we would have to be careful during the act of conception not to become too…er… too…'

Marcel gave her a rakish grin. 'Too what, Debbie?'

'Oh, Marcel! Don't tease me! You know perfectly well what I mean.'

'Too loving towards each other?'

She swallowed hard. 'Something like that. Only…'

'What you mean is, we mustn't fall in love.'

Dear Reader

The idea for my **French Hospital** duo came to me one hot summer day when I was picnicking with my ever-romantic husband among the sand dunes bordering one of my favourite French beaches. Not far from fashionable Le Touquet, and so quiet and tranquil, I decided that St Martin sur mer was the perfect setting for my two linked stories. That's not its real name, but perhaps if you visit the region and find yourself in a quaint little town with a hint of romance everywhere you explore, you may have found it.

A VERY SPECIAL BABY is the first book in this duo about two medical colleagues, Debbie and Jacky, both doctors, who become friends while working together at the Hôpital de la Plage. Romance blossoms for both of them amidst the energy of the Accident and Emergency Department.

I hope you enjoy reading these two books as much as I have enjoyed writing them.

Margaret Barker

In the second book, Jacky finds herself working alongside the charismatic Pierre Mellanger, her romantic idol from the past. Pierre broke Jacky's heart when she was younger because her love for him was unrequited. Dare she risk Pierre's rejection again?

Look out for Jacky's story, coming soon from Mills & Boon® Medical Romance™

A VERY
SPECIAL BABY

BY
MARGARET BARKER

MILLS & BOON®

All the characters in this book have no existence outside the imagination of the author, and have no relation whatsoever to anyone bearing the same name or names. They are not even distantly inspired by any individual known or unknown to the author, and all the incidents are pure invention.

First published in Great Britain 2005
Harlequin Mills & Boon Limited,
Eton House, 18-24 Paradise Road, Richmond, Surrey TW9 1SR

© Margaret Barker 2005

ISBN 0 263 84305 X

Set in Times Roman 10½ on 12 pt.
03-0505-48450

Printed and bound in Spain
by Litografia Rosés, S.A., Barcelona

CHAPTER ONE

'SO, HAVE you decided if we can have a baby sister like Céline's got, Mummy?'

Debbie handed her daughter a croissant as she considered the question that little Emma had first asked when she'd got in from her day at school last night. She was desperately wishing that she'd dealt with it immediately instead of being deliberately vague and changing the subject. Difficult subjects never got any easier if you shelved them. She should have learnt that lesson by now. Why hadn't she simply told the truth to her enquiring six-year-old?

Which was? Well, darling, Daddy walked out on us four years ago, and that put an end to Mummy's dream of having a large family. That's what she should have said. That would obviously have been too brutal for her little daughter. But it would have been the truth.

Paul had put paid to Debbie's long-cherished dream. But she'd have to wrap it up a bit and make the truth presentable. Even though Paul was a two-timing, not to be trusted individual, he was Emma's biological father and Debbie had made a point of never trying to influence the way her daughter thought about him.

Debbie picked up the milk bottle and topped up Emma's glass. 'Well, you see, it's like this, darling—'

'Mummy! You're pouring milk on the table!'

'Sorry!'

Debbie reached for a cloth. Anybody watching her now would think the child more capable than the mother. And to think that in half an hour's time she would be dealing with matters of life and death in Urgences, the accident and emergency department at the nearby Hôpital de la plage. But at least she'd had training before she'd qualified as a doctor, whereas she'd had absolutely no training to qualify her for her role as a single working mum. Apart from the example her super-efficient mother had set her. Somehow Debbie felt she would never be able to be as completely objective as her mother had been.

She put the milk bottle back in the fridge and rinsed out the cloth, keeping one eye on Emma to make sure she didn't drop apricot jam on her clean blouse. All she had to say now to Emma was that it would be impossible for Mummy to give her a baby sister because mummies needed daddies to make babies. Just say that and Emma would go off to school happy—well, not exactly happy but at least she would know the truth about the situation.

Returning to the table, Debbie reflected that Emma couldn't possibly realise how her innocent childish question had upset her last night. She didn't need to know that Debbie had lain awake half the night longing for a solution to the problem. At almost thirty years old she could hear the sound of her biological clock ticking away, and she desperately wanted another baby. She wanted Emma to have a sister or brother. She'd tried to shelve the idea but when Emma had brought up the subject it had touched a raw nerve.

Supposing, just supposing…would it be possible to have another baby without the hassle of a relationship? She didn't want a man! Never again! Not after Paul! But supposing…

Emma wriggled in her seat. 'Have you thought yet,

Mummy? You're taking a long time. Céline's got a lovely little sister and she didn't cost anything 'cos I asked her. She said her mummy just growed it in her tummy. I'd help you to look after it. And they don't eat much, do they?'

Debbie smiled as she stroked Emma's long blonde hair, making a mental note that it needed cutting again.

'You're quite right, babies don't eat much when they're small. Mummies do grow babies in their tummies but they need a daddy to help them to make the baby in the first place.'

'Why?'

Enquiring blue eyes stared up at her.

'Well, the daddy has to plant a seed in the mummy so that the baby will grow in her tummy.'

'You mean like when I helped you dig the garden and we put those grass seeds in and then we got some grass?'

'Something like that. Well, not exactly... Emma, it's quite complicated for a six-year-old to understand so I think we should talk about it when we've got more time. We have to leave in a few minutes. I've got to drive you to school and then go on to the hospital and—'

'I don't want another daddy 'cos I've got one, haven't I? And although I never see him, I've got his photo in my bedroom and he sends me lovely presents on my birthdays and at Christmas, doesn't he?'

Debbie reached forward and gave her daughter a hug. She smelled of fromage frais and croissants and there was a sticky patch of apricot jam on one side of her hair.

'Yes, Daddy loves you, darling,' Debbie said, trying hard to remain loyal to the image that Emma had of her father. 'Come on, let's go to the bathroom and get you cleaned up ready for school.'

'Can I wear my new jacket?'

'Of course you can. You're big enough to take care of your clothes now, aren't you?'

Debbie felt relieved that Emma had stopped asking awkward questions. Allowing her to wear the new jacket they'd bought in Le Touquet at the weekend would be a distraction. But as she supervised Emma's brushing of her teeth in the bathroom she found her mind dwelling on their conversation. One thing that had come out of it was that Emma didn't want another daddy. Well, that was definitely the end of it, then! Not that she'd ever considered the possibility of forming a long-term relationship with another man. Paul had put her off for life!

Leaving Emma at the door to her classroom, Debbie was once again relieved to find that her daughter ran towards her little French friends, chattering away to them as if she'd been born in France instead of London. But she'd made a point of speaking French to Emma when she was small just as her own French father had done with her when she'd spent time with him. It had been English at school and home with her mother, and French with her father and his family.

'*Au revoir, Maman!*' Emma trilled, turning to give a final wave.

'*Au revoir, chérie.*'

As Debbie drove along the coastal road that led to the Hôpital de la plage, she found herself relaxing again. No more difficult questions for a while! She loved this early morning drive along this stretch of the coast, with the sea dashing against the cliffs below her and on the other side of the road the picturesque green and brown, gently sloping hills. With the lovely April weather they'd been enjoying recently, the sheer beauty of this part of France always put her in a good mood and ready to start the day.

And she loved her work. Accident and Emergency departments here in France were much the same as in England. You never knew what was going to happen from one day to the next. It was challenging, exhilarating, sometimes exhausting but always very satisfying. Except when they lost a patient. Then you had to pick yourself up and try to remain detached. Keep a tight rein on your emotions. Over the years of her medical training and during her time as a qualified doctor she'd tried to learn how to do that. But sometimes she broke down—although never in front of the patients.

She waited until she got home. When Emma was asleep she would soak in the bath and have a quiet weep, at the same time telling herself there was nothing she could have done about it. She always wished she'd inherited her mother's tough personality. She'd never known her surgical consultant mother to worry about anything. She'd had to face up to the fact that basically she was a softie and there was nothing she could do about it. Her father had told her she took after him in personality. He was a softie, too, but he kept it well hidden, especially when he was performing a last-ditch, difficult operation to try to save a life which seemed doomed from the start.

And she'd inherited her father's dark hair. As a child she often wished she'd got her mother's blonde hair. When she'd been in her early teens she'd bought some blonde hair dye and given it a try. It had been a disaster, never to be repeated. And the streaky blonde hair had taken ages to grow out. Her own daughter had inherited the previously desired hair from her grandmother, reinforced by Paul's fair hair.

Driving down the hill towards St Martin sur mer, Debbie could see the whole bay spread out in front of her. The undulating sand-hills spilling down onto the beach and behind them the hotels, shops and houses. The hospital nestled at the bottom of the hill connected by a dual carriageway road to the nearby motorway. An ambulance was being driven at speed round the roundabout. Debbie held back, following it through the wide hospital gates before turning into the staff car park.

She squeezed into a space next to the one reserved for the consultant of Accident and Emergency. Climbing out, she was careful to hold onto her door so as not to scratch the flash car parked next to hers. Metallic silver, long sleek bonnet, sporty-looking thing it was. It was obvious that dear old Jacques Chantier had now retired. What a sweetie he'd been! So helpful when she'd first arrived here two years ago. A real warm-hearted family man. She couldn't have wished for a better boss to get her started in the French system. She'd been sorry to say goodbye to him yesterday.

Walking across to the entrance marked Urgences, she wondered fleetingly what the new consultant would be like. If he was anything like his car, he would be the exact opposite of Jacques! Jacques had driven the same old car for years, even though with his salary he could well have afforded a new one. She wasn't sure she was keen to meet this flash new consultant, but as long as he was good at his job she didn't care what he was like.

Glancing across at the hospital forecourt, she noticed a couple of patients being stretchered into Urgences from the ambulance she'd followed from the roundabout. Almost immediately a second ambulance arrived, followed closely by a third. She quickened her pace.

Closing the door of her locker, she unfolded the freshly laundered white coat and pulled it on, slinging her stethoscope round her neck.

'Venez ici, vite, vite, docteur!' called an imperious voice as soon as she arrived in the main reception area of Urgences.

She hurried across to the cubicle where the voice had demanded she arrive as soon as possible. A tall dark-haired man was securing an injured leg on a backslab. The white-faced patient lay motionless on the couch, seemingly barely conscious.

Debbie, not recognising the doctor attending him but noting the aura of authority surrounding him, surmised this had to be the new consultant. As he straightened up his white coat swung open, revealing an expensive-looking grey sharkskin jacket. The matching trousers were immaculately pressed. Not the usual run-of-the-mill, throw-on-the-first-thing-that-comes-to-hand-in-the-morning doctor she was accustomed to working with.

'Dehydration setting in, Doctor,' the new consultant told her tersely. 'Put in a line and get some dextrose into him. *Vite, vite!*'

Debbie reached for the sterile IV pack before beginning to ease back the patient's sleeve. She could see immediately that the forearm was swollen, and from the unnatural angle at which it was lying she deduced there was a fracture. Carefully she cut through the patient's shirtsleeve. He remained motionless as she worked, his eyes closed. At least he didn't appear to be in pain.

'We'll need a splint on here and an X-ray of the forearm,' Debbie said quietly in French, finding it perfectly natural to revert to her second language as she moved to the other side of the patient to fix up the IV. 'I'll see to that when I've got the dextrose flowing into the other arm. Has the patient been sedated?'

'The paramedics gave him some pethidine at the scene of the crash. I've arranged for him to go to Theatre as soon as he's been X-rayed. There's some internal damage, possibly the spleen…definitely something in the abdominal area. Haven't had time to do a full examination, as you can tell.'

'Do we know what happened?' Debbie said as she adjusted the flow of dextrose.

'Crash on the autoroute. Several cars and a lorry piled up. They're bringing in the casualties now. This man arrived first so I was able to see him quickly. I was told another doctor would be arriving soon, but I expected you would be here much sooner.'

Cool grey eyes surveyed her. 'I'm Marcel De Lange.'

'Debbie Sabatier.'

'Do you always arrive so late, Dr Sabatier?'

Debbie continued to fix the splint on the injured arm. Be polite was her motto when she was annoyed. She cleared her throat and began to speak in her best, much-practised Parisian accent that her father had told her would never fail to impress her seniors in the medical profession.

'I was actually early. I work set hours from nine till five.'

'How convenient for you.'

Debbie moved round the bed, taking care to give a wide berth to the consultant, who was still bending over their patient.

'It's written into my contract. You see, I have a child so I wouldn't want to work more hours.'

'Dr De Lange!'

A nurse poked her head around the door. 'Can you come and look at this patient, please, as soon as you've finished here?'

'Oui, j'arrive tout de suite.'

Marcel went over to the sink to wash his hands. 'I'll leave you to it, Dr Sabatier. Here are the patient's notes. He's still semi-conscious so we'd better have an X-ray of the skull. The name on the driving licence in his pocket is Bernard Dubois.'

As Marcel went out of the cubicle, the patient opened his eyes. 'What's happening now?'

Debbie leaned over her patient and smiled as she replied in French in a more friendly tone than she'd used with the difficult consultant. 'Good to hear you speaking at last. Can you tell me your name?'

'Bernard Dubois. What are my chances, Doctor?'

Debbie tried to reassure her patient, telling him that everything was under control and that he was going to be taken to X-Ray shortly. 'After we've decided what injuries you've sustained we'll—'

'You'll take me to Theatre. I know. I was listening to you and the other doctor talking, but I felt so sleepy I didn't want to be part of it. You seem to know what you're doing so I trust you, Doctor.'

Debbie smiled. 'Thanks.'

The patient gave a wan smile. 'Haven't much option, have I? Where do you come from, Doctor?'

'Good question. I lived most of my early life in London, but having a French father, I've also spent a lot of time in France.'

'Ah, that accounts for the touch of a foreign accent on certain words. I thought maybe you were French Canadian or perhaps Belgian.'

'No, I'm half English, half French.'

'So which country do you prefer to—?' The patient broke off, wincing with pain. 'My stomach feels like a herd of elephants have been stampeding over it. I heard the other doctor saying there's some abdominal damage.'

'We can't really tell until we've X-rayed you.'

'And opened me up. Oh, don't worry, I know the drill. I started medical school when I was eighteen. Flunked out at twenty-two. Couldn't stand the pace and being treated like a stupid schoolboy by the consultants. That was two years ago. I drive a lorry now and there's no hassle—but no prospects either. Ah, well, from what I've seen today I think I made the right career move. Wouldn't want all the aggro you doctors have to take. But I sometimes wish...'

'Dr Sabatier!'

Sister Marie Bezier hurried in and grabbed Debbie's arm. 'Dr De Lange needs you urgently. I'll stay with your patient.'

'How urgently?' Debbie asked, intent on fixing the arm splint before she left. She sometimes found that Marie was prone to exaggeration and Debbie always preferred to put the patient first.

'One of the casualties from the motorway crash is in labour. De Lange is furious that Obstetrics haven't taken her immediately. I think things are going to be different now we've got a dynamic consultant in charge. I'll finish that splint for you.'

Debbie downed tools and headed for the door. 'Thanks, Marie. I agree with you that things will never be the same again. We'll all wish dear old Jacques was back with us.'

'Oh, I don't know,' Marie said. 'Marcel De Lange is

such a handsome man, I don't mind how bossy he is. I like a man who's masterful. I've seen all the nurses drooling over him already.'

'Not interested,' Debbie said as she hurried away to find Marcel. She would be studiously professional and polite with him. But the less she saw of him the better. Handsome self-centred men were all the same. She should know! She'd been married to one of that diffi-cult-to-live-with species.

She found him in a nearby cubicle, leaning over a heavily pregnant woman obviously sedated or anaesthe-tised but completely motionless, her eyes closed.

'*Enfin!* At last!' he said as she went into the cubicle. 'I've alerted the obstetrics team.'

He lowered his voice. 'In the obstetrics department, they're currently delivering several babies simulta-neously apparently, including two sets of twins. How on earth they can—*Mon Dieu*…we can't wait any longer! Our patient has already signed a consent form for a Caesarean, should it be necessary. I've given her an epidural so she's not feeling any pain. Just look at the monitor!'

Marcel took Debbie to one side. 'Did you note the foetal distress?'

Debbie nodded. 'If we don't act quickly that baby will be—'

'Exactly! Scrub up quickly, Doctor. We can't risk losing that baby. Nurse, sterile gowns, please. Gloves, mask…'

Debbie had never prepared herself so quickly for a Caesarean section. She was standing on the other side of the treatment couch from Marcel De Lange, gowned, masked, gloved and ready in two minutes flat.

The nurse was swabbing the patient's abdomen in

preparation for surgery. She moved back as the consultant took his place and leaned over the patient.

'Have you any sensation below the waist, Sidonie?' he asked their patient.

'None whatsoever, Doctor. You go ahead and get my baby out, please.'

'You're a good patient. OK. Let's go ahead. Scalpel, Doctor...'

Marcel was holding out his hand, his eyes firmly fixed on the patient's enlarged abdomen. 'Come on, come on...'

Debbie handed over the sterile instrument.

Without hesitation he sliced through the skin, cutting into the abdominal tissue, skilfully negotiating the quickest way through to the uterus.

'Hold this muscle back with your retractors, Dr Sabatier. More retraction here! Yes, I can see now...'

Debbie breathed a sigh of relief as she watched him working. Knowing very little about him except that he was a consultant in emergency procedures, she'd worried that he might have only basic knowledge of obstetrics.

'You've done this before, haven't you?' she asked quietly, as she watched him slicing through the uterine wall.

'You didn't think I would endanger the patient if I hadn't, did you?' he snapped back.

'Sorry, I didn't mean—'

'Swab! Stem the blood flow. Over there, not here! That section where—'

'Sorry!' She leaned across.

'And stop saying sorry! Until I've got this... Ah!' He breathed a long sigh of relief as he lifted the baby through the uterine wall and out through the abdomen, handing its slippery body to Debbie, before commencing to suture the internal abdominal tissue.

As the baby was brought under the bright lights away from the warm dark comfort of its mother's womb, it gave a loud squawk of annoyance. Debbie smiled as she wrapped the squirming infant in a dressing sheet.

'You little darling,' she cooed in English. 'You don't like our bright noisy world, do you? Shall I put you back in your nest?'

Marcel continued to suture the uterine and surrounding abdominal tissue as he began to speak in perfectly correct but heavily accented English. 'You'd better not put him back, Doctor. Not after all the trouble we've gone to.'

So the man actually had a sense of humour! 'Dr De Lange says you've got to stay here, darling,' she whispered.

She gave the tiny infant to his mother for a brief cuddle. 'You've got a beautiful baby boy. I'm just going to clean him up a bit and then bring him back to you.'

She moved away to begin the postnatal checks, placing the baby boy on a sterile sheet as she began by clearing his nostrils to ensure a clear airway. As she worked she talked quietly to him in French, loving every second of being able to handle this tiny precious infant.

Marcel looked up as he finished the external suturing.

'When you're ready, Doctor,' he said, reverting to rapid French again. 'Sidonie, would you like to hold him again before we do any more postnatal checks?'

The happy mother held out her arms for her baby.

'There you go, Sidonie,' Debbie said. 'Your beautiful little boy. He weighs three kilos and he's perfectly formed.'

Debbie handed over the newborn, making sure that the mother was strong enough to hold him in her arms for longer than a few seconds.

The mother's eyes were wet with tears as she hugged her baby son close to her breast. 'He's beautiful. Robert wanted a son. I didn't mind so long as our baby was healthy.'

Debbie turned away. She could feel tears pricking in her own eyes as she watched the young mother with her much-loved son. Oh, how she would love another baby! But it wasn't to be, so she'd better get used to the idea and stop wishing for the moon.

Unknown to Debbie, Marcel was watching her display of emotion. For an instant he felt unnerved by what he saw. Had he been too harsh with this English doctor? Was that why she was looking so upset? She was undoubtedly a very capable doctor. She'd been an asset to him as he'd worked to deliver the baby.

The door opened and a tall young doctor arrived. 'We can take your patient to Obstetrics now, Dr De Lange so...'

The young man's voice trailed away. 'Ah, I see the baby's here already. We hadn't realised the birth was imminent or we...'

Marcel took the young doctor on one side and spoke quietly. 'The baby was in great distress. Without an immediate Caesarean we would have lost him. It's fortunate I'm an experienced surgeon who's worked in obstetrics otherwise...'

He spread his hands as if to emphasise how grave the danger would have been.

'I'll arrange to have Sidonie and her baby transferred to your care now, Doctor,' Marcel continued with steely calm. 'But I will be monitoring the progress of these patients. She is to stay in the preliminary obstetrics ward next door until I'm satisfied that she is ready to go to the main obstetrics ward.'

'Yes, sir. I will explain this to my consultant as soon as—'

'You do that.'

Marcel turned away from the nervous young doctor and smiled down at his patient. 'We're going to have you transferred now to the preliminary obstetrics ward.'

Sidonie put out her hand and placed it on Marcel's arm. 'Will you come in and see us, Doctor? You've been so good to me. I don't know what I would have done without you.'

'Of course I will. You'll be right next door.'

'I shouldn't really have been driving, with the baby due next week. But I wanted to see my mother today and…well, when that car pulled out in front of me I thought that was the end! Have you phoned my husband?'

'He's on his way back from Paris,' the consultant said gently. 'Now, try to relax, Sidonie. I'll come in and see you later.'

He turned to look at Debbie. 'That's one good thing about this hospital. The preliminary units attached to Urgences are a great asset. It does mean we can liaise with the medical staff who take over from us. That way we can follow their initial progress before they're taken to the bigger wards.'

'Is that the only good thing about this hospital?' Debbie asked, recognising Marcel's undertones of discontent.

He raised an eyebrow as he looked down at her. 'I hope there are more good points, but at the moment I've yet to discover them.'

'Doctor for cubicle four!' called one of the nurses. 'As quick as you can make it...please!'

It was several hours before all the casualties of the motorway crash had been taken care of. Six patients had been transferred to the preliminary wards and two were still in Theatre, Bernard Dubois being one of them.

On the instructions of Marcel, Debbie had kept in touch with Theatre and given the consultant a continuous report on Bernard's progress.

'The prognosis seems promising,' she told Marcel as she put her last written report on the desk in the consultant's office situated at the side of Urgences.

Marcel looked up from his desk. He'd only just sat down for the first time for several hours and the mound of paperwork looked uninviting to say the least. He was a hands-on doctor and disliked the inevitable paperwork.

He stood up. 'I'll deal with that later when I've found where my secretary is hiding.'

'She works in your consulting rooms next to the outpatients department where you see patients and their relatives who've asked for a consultation with you.'

'Well, she'll have to come and work here.'

Marcel picked up the most recent report Debbie had placed on his desk, running his eyes down the page. 'I'm glad Bernard is surviving well in Theatre. Complicated case. When we have orthopaedic injuries combined with abdominal injuries it's never easy for the medical staff or the patient. Please, continue to keep me informed of Bernard's progress.'

She hesitated. 'I'm afraid I'm off duty now...well, since ten minutes ago. My little girl will be waiting for me at home, you see.'

'Ah, yes, I'd forgotten you have a family. Well, run along, then. Don't keep them all waiting.'

As she went out of the door she heard him call her back. 'Debbie! I may call you Debbie, may I?' He was speaking in his charmingly accented English again.

'Of course, if I can call you Marcel.'

He smiled. 'That goes without saying,' he continued in English.

Debbie smiled back. The ice was beginning to thaw. The great man was human after all! She'd begun to think he was as human as a machine.

Encouraged by his more relaxed tone, she decided to ask the question she hadn't dared ask before. 'Where did you learn to speak English, Marcel?'

'I worked for a year in an English hospital.' He hesitated. 'And I was married to an English woman for a couple of years.'

The smile had vanished from his face. It was as if the shutters had been pulled down to obscure the sunshine. Debbie sensed that their short friendly chat was over. She turned.

'*A demain.* See you tomorrow, Debbie,' he said as she moved away.

'*A demain*, Marcel.'

As he watched Debbie go, he was wondering again if he'd been too harsh with her. He was always strict with his staff at the beginning of a new job where he was in charge. It was essential to show everybody that he wouldn't allow his exacting standards to slip. But Debbie had probably found him particularly difficult.

He didn't want to alienate her. She was an excellent doctor. And as a family woman she didn't pose a threat. Married women were strictly off limits to him. He couldn't deny that he'd found her attractive, but after the trauma of Lisa's betrayal and his acrimonious divorce he was extremely wary of attractive women.

Her shoulder-length dark hair, which she'd coiled up before putting it into her theatre cap, looked soft and silky. And he couldn't help noticing the fluid movement of her body as she made her way through Urgences. Beneath that white coat she had a slim sexy figure...

No! He checked his train of thought. As a married woman she was out of bounds to him so he'd better continue with the professional stance he'd set up.

But there was no harm in being a bit more friendly than he had been. A bit of friendliness couldn't possibly lead anywhere. And he sensed that Debbie would be fun to get to know—but only as a friend. He was used to ignoring his natural emotional responses since Lisa had deceived him. Life had become much easier since he'd given up on deep feelings. No woman would ever hurt him again as Lisa had. The emotional wounds were healing but the scars remained.

Debbie quickened her step, somehow sensing that the new consultant was watching her. The brief thaw in their relations had allowed her a glimpse of the real man. Beneath that façade of superiority he was probably a warm-blooded individual. She wondered why his two-year marriage had ended. His wife may have died. He'd certainly looked sad when he spoke about the marriage.

She tried hard to put him out of her mind as she headed for the medical staff locker room, but something about him had gripped her imagination. She'd found him demanding to work with, but she admired his skills and judgement of a case. He was without doubt an excellent doctor and sometimes people who excelled in their profession could be very exacting. They expected high standards. That wouldn't be a problem for her. She aspired always to do the best she could.

Maybe she would learn to enjoy working with Marcel, she thought as she slammed the locker shut and turned the key. Walking out to her car, she found herself hoping that Marcel wouldn't be so exacting tomorrow. All work and no play. She'd like him to lighten up a little during the day. Smile more perhaps? Yes, he had a fabulous smile. When he'd smiled just now it had transformed his undoubtedly handsome face.

She'd noticed his dazzling white teeth positively shining between his lips. She opened the car door and climbed in, still thinking about that smile. Inserting the key into the ignition, she remembered in particular his lips. Wide, luscious, sexy... Ah, now, that was where she really must call a halt to thinking about Marcel De Lange. It was enough that she'd discovered he was human, without endowing him with attributes she didn't want to know about.

Emma rushed out through the door as soon as Debbie pulled into the short semi-circular drive in front of their little house.

'Mummy, Mummy, Francoise has made some *pomme frites* for my supper. Come and have some with me.'

Debbie hugged her daughter. As they went into the house together Debbie was thinking what a treasure Francoise had turned out to be. She lived in the village and had been acting as part-time mother's help for Debbie ever since she'd moved there two years ago. A widow in her early fifties, her own children had grown up and she seemed to enjoy looking after Emma, meeting the school bus in the village to bring her home and looking after her until Debbie arrived. She would babysit if Debbie went out or was called in to work on a major emergency at the hospital.

Automatically, Debbie and Emma reverted to French as they went into the kitchen because Francoise spoke very little English.

'*Bonsoir*, Debbie.' Francoise turned round from the sink, wiping her hands down her apron. '*Ça va?*'

'*Oui, ça va bien.* I'm fine, thank you. *Et vous*, Francoise?'

'I've had a good day. And Emma has been helping me to prepare supper. *Voulez-vous du jambon avec les pommes frites?*'

Debbie said ham and chips would be lovely. Francoise was only supposed to make supper for Emma, but she usually made far too much for one small child. If Debbie was hungry, as she was today, not having had time to take a lunch-break, an early supper was most welcome. Especially placed on the kitchen table as Francoise was doing now.

There was a huge bowl of *pommes frites*, a large serving dish of ham and a bowl of salad.

'May I toss the salad, *Maman*?' Emma asked, picking up the large wooden salad servers.

'Of course you may. I'll hold the bowl. Francoise, are you sure you won't join us? Let me get another plate.'

'No, I've got to get back. My son's coming round to fix some shelves for me this evening. *Bon appetit!*'

'*Merci,*' Debbie said, one hand holding the salad bowl and the other holding the back of Emma's sweater as she stood on the kitchen chair, leaning over the table.

Emma and Debbie said their goodbyes to Francoise as she left them. As soon as she'd gone they both reverted to English again.

'I'm glad you're home, Mummy,' Emma said as she sank back onto her chair, placing the servers back in the well-tossed salad and wiping a smear of vinaigrette down one side of her chubby cheek. 'I wish my daddy would come to supper some time. Why doesn't he come to see us?'

Here we go again! Debbie swallowed a chip and looked across the table at her daughter.

'Daddy lives a long way across the sea in America. He's a very busy man and he can't get away from his work at the hospital.'

'But he still loves me, doesn't he?'

'Of course he does, darling.'

'Well, that's OK then.' Emma chewed her chips happily. 'We don't need to get another daddy, do we?'

'No, we don't.'

Absolutely not! Meeting Marcel De Lange and observing his arrogance had somehow reminded her of the first time she'd met Paul. They were similar types. She couldn't imagine ever being persuaded into thinking Marcel would be a warm-hearted man.

And yet there was something dangerously and undeniably attractive about him. Some aspect of his personality that she didn't want to dwell on. Good thing she was only interested in him from a professional point of view. Although, if she was honest, if she hadn't promised herself she would never get hurt again, she wouldn't mind spending some time with him. But a man like that could reduce her to an emotional wreck just as Paul had done.

Sometimes she really felt she'd recovered emotionally from the way he'd behaved and then something would happen to remind her and she'd find herself back

at square one. No, she wasn't going down that road
again ever!

'Can I have some more *pommes frites*, Mummy?'

Debbie smiled as she picked up the serving spoon.
Emma was all she needed...except she'd love another
baby. But for that she needed a man...

CHAPTER TWO

AFTER working with Marcel for a couple of weeks, Debbie found she was becoming more relaxed with him. As she flicked through the notes that had landed up on her desk in her tiny office near the end of the main reception area, she realised that the feeling of apprehension that had haunted her for the first couple of days since the consultant's arrival had vanished.

It had also helped that Marcel seemed more relaxed when he was working. Maybe he'd been as nervous as the rest of them when he'd first arrived and had been putting on an act to show them all he meant business. Well, whatever the reason, he was much more approachable now, thank goodness!

She had to reread the letter she'd been skimming because her thoughts had been elsewhere. She looked up as somebody tapped on her door before coming in. She could feel an unwelcome heightening of the colour in her cheeks as she saw the man she'd been thinking about standing in front of her desk.

He put his hands on the desk and leaned forward. 'I'm having a house-warming party tomorrow night. I wondered if you and your husband would like to join us.'

'A house-warming?'

Marcel raised an eyebrow at her surprised tone of voice. 'And what's so strange about that? It's my way of getting to know my medical colleagues better than it's possible when we're all working together.'

So he was mellowing! 'Yes, it sounds like an excellent idea.' She cleared her throat. 'I wouldn't bring my husband if I were able to come. We're divorced. My ex-husband lives in America so as a single parent it's difficult for me to get out in the evenings.'

Marcel chose to ignore the uplifting of his spirits when he heard Debbie say she was divorced. He'd already enquired about her marital status but wanted to make quite sure he hadn't been misinformed. He was trying to convince himself that, although he was intrigued by Debbie and would like to get to know her, he could handle and ignore any emotional feelings that might threaten to complicate their friendship.

She was an interesting woman, an intelligent and experienced colleague, and he would value her friendship—nothing more, apart from the fact that she was very easy on the eye.

Watching her arrive through the main door of Urgences this morning, he hadn't been able to help noticing the way her slim hips had moved beneath her well-fitting trouser suit. She'd looked very competent, ready to deal with any emergency, but delightfully feminine and sexy at the same time. He admired her as a woman—a very feminine, attractive woman—but he was sure he could keep his instinctive desires under control.

He switched from French to English. 'Ah, so we're both in the same boat, as you English say. I'm divorced, too.'

Debbie looked across her desk into the cool grey eyes, but Marcel was giving nothing away. Neither was she. She made a point of remaining emotionally detached when she told people she was divorced. She didn't want anyone to know how she'd felt as if her heart had been ripped out when she'd discovered Paul's treachery.

'I don't go out much in the evenings,' she said quietly. 'Thanks for the invitation, but I'm sorry—I can't come.'

Marcel shifted his hands so that he could perch on the end of Debbie's desk.

'You mean you have a previous engagement?'

It was obvious she hadn't by the guilty look on her face, but he wanted to hear what she would say. Debbie was a woman who wasn't accustomed to lie, so different to Lisa who had got lying and deceit down to a fine art before their divorce.

Debbie hesitated, wondering whether to say she already had a social arrangement and that would be the end of it. She wouldn't feel comfortable doing that but on the other hand…

'Why do I get the impression you don't want to come?' Marcel said as he waited for her reply.

'Well, I'd need to get a babysitter for Emma and—'

'Is that a problem? Don't you ever go out by yourself?'

'Of course I do! I come to the hospital, don't I?'

'All work and no play makes…'

She looked down at her papers, unable to stand the eye contact with this devastatingly handsome and very persistent man.

'Yes, I know. Well, I used to get out more, but lately…'

'It's only a gathering of people from Urgences, not a ball. Eight o'clock till eleven. Come as you are. Dress code optional. The people on call will probably be back in the hospital by eleven and those who've been working since dawn will be falling asleep. My place is just around the corner a little way up the hill, so it's very convenient for those who are on call to nip back.'

'Well…'

'How old is your daughter?' Marcel said, with an air of exasperation.

Debbie smiled. 'Emma's six.'

'No problem with a babysitter, then. I'm sure you can arrange it…if you want to.' He stood up. 'I just think it would be a good idea to get as many of my staff who are working together in a social situation. Now that I know what you're all like professionally, I'd like to get to know everybody in a relaxed atmosphere.'

'So you've decided we're all OK professionally, then?'

'I didn't say that. I'm still reserving judgement on some members of staff.'

'Are you reserving judgement on me, Marcel?'

As he smiled down at her, Debbie felt a distinct quickening of her pulse. Probably just an illusion, but a wide sexy smile like that would have been her undoing at one time. Since Paul had taught her the danger of becoming emotionally involved only to be disillusioned, she hadn't allowed herself to give in to her natural emotional responses.

'I'm particularly reserving judgement on you, Debbie.'

She repressed a shiver as she listened to his deep gravelly voice. Was she imagining it or had Marcel implied a *double entendre* in that last statement?

He turned away and headed for the door. 'You're needed in X-Ray, Debbie. The nurse who took your patient there would like further instructions for when his X-ray is completed.'

'I'm on my way.'

He held open the door and they walked back into the main reception area.

'Let me know what you decide about tomorrow night,' he said, lightly, as she headed off towards X-Ray.

'As I told you, I'll need to get a babysitter, but I'll get back to you as soon as possible.'

'Marcel!' Sister Marie came hurrying across. 'Can you come and see this patient now?'

As Marcel went across to the cubicle where Marie was working, he found himself thinking that Debbie was making unnecessary excuses. She probably hadn't forgiven him for the way he'd treated her on his first day here. Well, he didn't really care if she couldn't come, he told himself. Perhaps it would be for the best now that he'd discovered she was divorced.

Debbie went along to X-Ray to find out what the problem was. She'd already given her instructions to the nurse, but she was inexperienced and needed reassurance. After that, she headed off to the preliminary orthopaedic unit to see Bernard. Marcel had asked if she would check on their emergency patient and, two weeks on from his traffic accident, arrange for him to be moved to the main orthopaedic ward.

Debbie found their patient propped up against his pillows, reading a copy of *Le Figaro*.

'Nothing but gloom and doom in here,' Bernard said. 'I'm feeling utterly depressed. It's good to see you, Debbie, but I hope you've come to cheer me up.'

'Do you want the good news or the bad news, Bernard?' Debbie said in French.

'The good news, of course.'

'Well, the good news is you've been making good

progress. The bad news is you may be in hospital for longer than we first anticipated.'

Bernard shrugged. 'That's no bad thing. I've got nothing much to go back to. Apart from the pain, the bossy nurses and doctors, the awful food, the lack of available girls and all the rest of it…at least I'm alive, they've decided not to chop my leg off and I'm almost contemplating swallowing my pride and applying to go back to medical school should I ever be allowed out of here.'

'Well, good for you! I know which I'd rather do, drive a lorry or work in a hospital. I mean, we all get bad days when we're still medical students, the lowest of the low, but rise above it, stick it out and it's well worth the aggro. Believe me, I've had no regrets—recently,' she added with a self-deprecating laugh.

'Keep telling me while I'm in here, Debbie. You're one of my role models. The other is Marcel De Lange. He's quite something, isn't he? I mean, he's got everything hasn't he? Good looks, a brilliant mind, good surgical skills…'

There was a cough behind her. 'Is somebody talking about me?'

Debbie turned to find Marcel standing behind her, having arrived unnoticed through the side door of the preliminary unit close to Bernard's bed.

'Bernard was telling me he's thinking about going back to medical school when he gets out of here because he thinks you and I enjoy our work at the hospital.'

'Good idea, Bernard! If there's anything I can do to help you…'

'Thank you, sir. If you could bring me a few textbooks. Perhaps something about orthopaedics. Having smashed up the tibia and fibula in my leg, the radius and ulna in my arm, not to mention four ribs, I think I might make a good sympathetic orthopaedic surgeon.'

'It's possible,' Marcel said. 'What's happened to your old medical books?'

Bernard gave a sheepish grin. 'I made a funeral pyre when I quit medical school and burned them all so I couldn't change my mind.'

Marcel smiled. 'I felt like doing that during my training but I'm glad I didn't. I'll find you some books you might find useful. Now, let's look at the latest report on the ultrasound scan of your abdomen.'

Marcel fixed the film of the scan into the light-box on the wall. 'We decided the spleen was viable in spite of the damage, and I think we were right. There is obvious regeneration already. Good! As you know, Bernard, we thought about doing a splenectomy but we gambled that with a young fit man like you we might get away with more conservative treatment. And we did. So don't let us down now. Do everything we tell you. Oh, and keep reading the textbooks on orthopaedics when I give them to you. Maybe I'll spring a test on you one of these days.'

Bernard laughed. 'Marcel, you're a slave-driver.'

'I know, but it will keep you out of mischief.'

'What mischief could I possibly get up to in here? No girls—apart from Debbie—and she's happily married.'

'No, I'm not,' Debbie said, regretting immediately how she'd set the record straight. 'That is to say, I'm divorced, but I'm as good as married because I'm totally devoted to my daughter and intend to spend the rest of my life as a single mother.'

'How boring!' Bernard said. 'You're much too young

and attractive to stay single. Marcel, tell Debbie to snap out of it and start living a little.'

Marcel shrugged. 'Debbie is very independent. I've been trying to get her to come to my house-warming party tomorrow but it's one excuse after another so…'

'Oh, Debbie, it's only a party!' Bernard said.

'OK, I'll come! If I can get a babysitter.'

Both Marcel and Bernard groaned. 'Excuses, excuses, excuses…'

'No it's not. Anyway, we're going to have to move you to the main orthopaedic ward, Bernard. I'm going to arrange that now with the orthopaedic firm.'

'That will be a good move for your future career,' Marcel said. 'If you ask a lot of questions you'll gain valuable experience while you're waiting for your bones to heal.'

Bernard frowned. 'I don't want to leave here but so long as you two come in and see me now and again, I'll be happy.'

As soon as she got home, Debbie asked Francoise about babysitting for Marcel's house-warming party. Francoise was delighted to be asked.

'It's ages since I sat in for you during the evening, Debbie. I was only saying to my daughter yesterday that you don't get out enough. I know you're out at the hospital all day but that's work. And Emma will be OK with me, darling, won't you?'

Emma smiled. 'Will you give me another cookery lesson, Francoise?'

'*Eh bien, chérie, Maman* isn't going out until half past seven so you will already be in bed, won't you?'

'Francoise, it will be Friday night. No school on Saturday so I can stay up late.'

Emma looked at Debbie. 'I can stay up late at the weekend, can't I? You always let me, *Maman*.'

Debbie looked at the other woman who was nodding her assent. Francoise loved spending time with Emma. It reminded her of the days when she'd been so important to her two sons and two daughters. Now that they were independent she found she very much missed the enthusiasm and innocence of young children. And the generous wages that Debbie insisted on paying her for looking after Emma were an added bonus.

Debbie put an arm around her daughter's shoulders. 'OK, you can stay up late, but you must go to bed as soon as Francoise asks you to.'

'*Bien sûr, Maman!*'

The next evening Debbie was plunged into indecision as to what she should wear. It had to be something casual but nothing inappropriate. She wanted to look cool, as if she went out into Le Touquet every night and spent her weekends in Paris. In the end she chose the expensive designer jeans she'd splashed out on when she'd been in Paris, visiting her father and his family the previous summer.

Louise, her father's wife, who was the epitome of Parisian chic, had told her the jeans accentuated her slim figure. If she teamed them with her new floaty chiffon blouse, the outfit would hopefully look like something from the fashion page in the women's magazine she'd bought last Saturday.

Why she was getting so nervous or making such an effort she couldn't imagine. It had nothing to do with Marcel, of course! she thought as she carefully applied her make-up and then wiped it all off so she could redo it.

Downstairs, she could hear Francoise and Emma chattering in French and laughing as they put out the ingredients for the *tarte aux pommes* they were going to make. Marcel had been quite right when he'd accused her of making an excuse so that she wouldn't have to go to his house-warming party. There was nothing to be afraid of.

Except herself! Her own fear of relaxing again in a party situation. Of admitting to herself that it was time she got a life of her own and stopped pretending that being a single mum was the only kind of emotion she required to stay happy. OK, maybe she would relax her rules a bit tonight, but only slightly. Nobody—and especially somebody like Marcel—was ever going to break through her emotional barrier again.

As she pulled a jacket over her floaty blouse and headed for the door, she told herself she was fully prepared for an enjoyable evening. Friendship, that was all she needed. All she would allow herself if she wanted to prevent ever being disillusioned again.

Downstairs, she hugged Emma and thanked Francoise for all her help.

Francoise lifted her hands from the large mixing bowl. 'Now, you enjoy yourself, Debbie. And don't hurry back. Jérome will wait for you if you're not ready when he gets there.'

'You're sure I'm not imposing on your son by...'

Francoise smiled as she dusted some flour from her hands. 'It was my idea wasn't it? No, not too much water in the pastry, Emma...*doucement, ma chérie. Oui, c'est ca. Parfait!*'

Debbie felt decidedly redundant as Francoise began walking to the front door with her.

'There's Jérome now. He enjoys a drive out in the

evenings in his uncle's car. He never touches alcohol but I know you doctors enjoy a glass of wine when you're off duty. And quite right, too, after all the horrors you have to deal with during the day. So let your hair down, Debbie, and enjoy yourself. And don't worry about Emma because it's a real joy for me to have her to myself for the evening.'

Jérome was climbing out of the car and coming round to open the passenger door. The idea of being chauffeured there and back had been entirely Francoise's idea, but Debbie had insisted she must pay full taxi rates for the privilege. She knew that Jérome didn't earn very much over at his uncle's farm on the edge of the village. It was a family arrangement whereby the nephew got his board and lodgings and a small wage in exchange for help with the cows, pigs and general farm maintenance.

'*Bonsoir*, Debbie,' Jérome said.

'*Bonsoir*, Jérome.'

Debbie climbed into the front passenger seat, settling herself against the ancient leather.

They chatted about the unseasonally warm early May weather as they drove along the coast road and then the conversation dried up. Debbie was happy simply to look out over the moonlit sea. She wound down her window so that she could imagine the salty scent of the waves below her. When the hot summer weather really arrived, she would take Emma swimming. Last year she'd taught her to swim during the hot summer months, but the water had been too cold during the winter and she'd rarely got around to taking her to the swimming pool in St Martin sur mer.

'That's the house up there above the hospital,' she told Jérome as they approached the roundabout.

'Nice house. Expensive,' Jérome said. 'Your boss is he, this man?'

'Yes, he's the medical consultant in Urgences.'

'Married, is he?' Jérome asked as he drove into the semi-circular drive.

'I believe he's divorced or something,' Debbie said in a vague tone, anxious to get off the subject of Marcel.

'Could be worth getting to know,' Jérome said dryly as he cast his eye over the large stone house, illuminated as if for a *son et lumière* performance.

'You should know by now I'm not the least bit interested in men,' Debbie said as she climbed out of the car.

Jérome grinned. 'Maybe you should be. Now, you take your time, Debbie. I'm going over to see my girlfriend in Montreuil sur mer, but I'll come back in good time. Eleven o'clock you said, didn't you? Sure you don't want to make it twelve. I don't mind.'

'Eleven will be fine, thank you.'

'Debbie! Come in!' Marcel greeted her as she stepped into the spacious entrance hall.

A Mozart concerto was playing softly in the background. The hall was crowded with colleagues talking noisily and laughing loudly.

'It's just like a normal day in Urgences without the patients,' Marcel said. 'Let me take your jacket. Come through to the kitchen for a drink.'

'Lovely blouse!' Marie said, as Debbie passed her in the terracotta-tiled corridor leading to the kitchen.

'Thanks. I couldn't decide what to wear so...'

'Oh, you always look good in whatever you're wearing. Wish I had your figure.'

Debbie began to relax. She'd made good friends since

she'd started working in Urgences. There was no reason why she shouldn't count Marcel as one of them. There was no need for her to regard him with suspicion. And yet she always found she was holding herself in check whenever she was with him.

But as he handed her a glass of champagne in the kitchen she had to admit she found him attractive in a dangerous sort of way. Perhaps the danger she felt at approaching this friendship helped to heighten the sense of adventure she experienced whenever she was with him.

He was such a vibrant character. He intrigued her with his air of mystery. Well, whatever it was, she was going to enjoy herself this evening. Looking around the huge farmhouse-type kitchen, she reckoned there must be about twenty people crammed in there. She'd worked with all of them at one time or another, which made for an easygoing atmosphere.

A small pretty nurse, newly arrived in the department, approached them.

'Marcel, I wanted to ask you about that patient who came in this afternoon. The lady with the—'

'Sorry Veronique, no talking shop tonight. Come and see me tomorrow morning. Would you like another glass of champagne?'

Veronique smiled a dazzling smile as she accepted. She hadn't really wanted to ask about the patient but thought it would be a good way of getting herself noticed by her highly desirable boss.

Debbie wandered through into the sitting room where another crowd had gathered. Somebody had changed the music to a lively more up-to-date piece they could dance to. Debbie wasn't sure what it was but it was certainly getting people onto their feet. Some were making a valiant attempt to dance gracefully while others seemed to enjoy making fools of themselves occasionally, laughing at the same time as they all enjoyed the relaxation from their busy working lives.

She recognised Pierre Lamentier, the usually straight-faced obstetrics consultant, jacket flung over a chair, smiling happily as he danced vigorously with a junior midwife.

Debbie danced for a while with various colleagues until she excused herself, saying she needed a break. It was at that point that she realised she was looking around in the hope of seeing what Marcel was up to. She could see him now, in the centre of an admiring group as he recounted some story which had them all in fits of laughter.

She turned away, thinking this was a good time for some refreshment from the cold buffet that Marcel had told her about. In the impressive high-ceilinged dining room she helped herself to the cold meats and salad set out on a large round table in the centre of the room. She chatted with a couple of nurses from Urgences as they sat together until they were ready to go back and join the others.

She paused as she was leaving the dining room, turning back to have one last glimpse of the magnificent sea view. The lights from the town illuminated the seashore and she could see myriad twinkling lights shining from the boats moored close to shore. Such a beautiful house! She was enjoying the relative calm here in the dining room but it was time to go back and mingle with the other guests.

'Ah, there you are!' Marcel said as he walked through the door.

'I was just admiring the view. You've got a superb situation here.'

He smiled down at her. 'I love living near the sea.'

'So do I.'

Marcel was so close now she could smell the scent of his aftershave. Something distinctively attractive in a very masculine kind of way.

'Everything OK at home when you left? Not worried about your babysitter, are you?'

'Oh, Francoise is an absolute treasure. I don't know what I'd do without her.'

'And she didn't mind putting in the overtime?'

'Quite the reverse. She loves to come in the evening whenever I…'

Her voice trailed away as she watched the amused smile on Marcel's face.

'So, your original excuse about getting a babysitter was…'

She felt her colour rising. 'OK, yes, I freely admit it was an excuse. But when you've been badly let down and have gone through an acrimonious divorce, you tend to keep yourself to yourself.'

She looked up into Marcel's concerned eyes and saw real sympathy there. She couldn't think why she was saying all this to him.

'I'm sorry, I don't know why I'm telling you this in the middle of your party. You should be mixing with your guests, not listening to my problems.'

He put a hand on her arm and smiled down at her. 'Believe me, I know exactly what you mean. I've been in the same situation myself. You feel as if you'll never be able to face social situations again, don't you?'

She nodded, still mesmerised by the sympathetic expression in Marcel's grey eyes. 'Somehow I didn't think you were a fellow sufferer. You always seem so together.'

He laughed and the tense atmosphere was dispelled. 'I'm a good actor. Sometimes I think I've missed my vocation. Let me top up your glass, Debbie.'

He was reaching for a bottle from a nearby table. 'Are you driving?'

'No, I've got a friend picking me up at eleven.'

'Alors, encore de champagne pour madame?'

'Mais oui, s'il vous plaît.' She realised she needed something to stop her emotions from churning when she was close to Marcel.

'I'm glad you helped yourself to the buffet,' Marcel said as he poured her champagne. 'Everybody's having supper when they feel like it. Those on call had an early supper so they wouldn't miss out if there's an emergency.'

He paused. 'Are you coming back into the sitting room now?'

He put a hand under her arm. She enjoyed the feeling of being escorted by her host. That's all he was. The host politely escorting one of his guests, she told herself as they went back into the noisy sitting room.

She watched Marcel as he set off round the room carrying a couple of bottles, topping up glasses as he went. There was champagne for the lucky ones who weren't driving or on call, and fizzy water or fruit juice for the rest.

Debbie struck up a conversation with a group of colleagues and soon found she was enjoying being in such a relaxed atmosphere. It was the first time since her divorce that she'd begun to feel as if her old self was returning. But she realised that the best part of the evening was when she'd been with Marcel. She'd accepted that he was only playing the dutiful host, as he did with everyone else, but it made her feel special.

Just before eleven she went across the room to speak to him. 'I'd better get my jacket. My lift will be here soon,' she told him.

His eyes flickered. 'Pity you can't stay longer.'

'That would have been nice but…'

'I know, you want to get back to your daughter. Oh, well, perhaps we could have a drink together some time soon.'

'I'd like that,' she said, toning down the eagerness she felt at the prospect. Her mobile rang. 'It's Jérome, my driver. I wonder what he wants.'

'Perhaps he's been delayed,' Marcel said, hoping that this would be the case.

Debbie listened to Jérome apologising that he was going to have to mend a flat tyre so he would be a bit late. As she cut the connection she looked up at Marcel.

'Is there a problem?' he asked.

'Jérome's car has a flat tyre. He's been out to see his girlfriend in Montreuil sur mer and is coming back over the hill. He says it shouldn't take long to mend. I'd better phone Francoise to say we'll be late.'

'Excuse me a moment. Got to say goodbye to a few people.' Marcel drifted off.

As Debbie phoned Francoise, she could see that most people were already leaving. Some colleagues had been called back to the hospital, others, tired from a busy day's work, were heading home.

'Francoise, *c'est* Debbie.' Quickly, she explained the problem, assuring her that there was nothing to worry about.

Francoise said she was falling asleep on the sofa. Did Debbie mind if she went upstairs to sleep in the guest bedroom? She would be near Emma's room if the little girl needed anything.

Debbie said of course she didn't mind. It was a good idea. As she cut the connection, she wished she'd suggested it earlier. Francoise had stayed the night sometimes before when Debbie had occasionally been called in for an emergency situation at the hospital.

Marcel returned and looked at her enquiringly. 'Everything OK at home?'

'Yes. Francoise is going to spend the night with us as she sometimes does.'

'That's nice. So you can stay as long as it takes for your driver to get here.'

She swallowed hard. 'Oh, Jérome will turn up as soon as he's mended that puncture.'

'Well, make yourself at home while I see everybody off.'

She sank down on the sofa, suddenly getting that nervous feeling again. Marcel was obviously being very polite to her. He didn't seem at all put out by the fact that one of his guests was going to be hanging around after everyone else had gone. In fact, he seemed positively pleased. Maybe he was! The thought made her pulse race. She mustn't allow herself to think of Marcel as anybody other than a friend. That was the way she was going to play it with him. Because she knew deep down she fancied him rotten! And that was where the problem lay.

'They've all gone.'

At the sound of Marcel's voice Debbie opened her eyes. She was leaning back against the soft cushions and he was sitting at the other end of the sofa.

She rubbed her eyes. 'I must have fallen asleep. What time is it?'

'Half past eleven. I've brought you some coffee to revive you.'

'Thanks.'

She took the thin porcelain cup from his hands. As their hands touched she felt a shiver of desire running down her spine and knew she was in a dangerous situation, the sort of situation she'd avoided for a long time and should have avoided now.

The most sensible course of action would have been to tell Jérome she would call a taxi. Why hadn't she done that? But, looking across the length of the sofa at the handsome man who was watching her with an enigmatic expression, she couldn't help feeling glad that she'd stayed.

CHAPTER THREE

DEBBIE took a sip of her coffee to steady her nerves. 'Jérome's taking a long time mending that puncture. I think I'll ring him and see how he's getting on. I could always take a taxi.'

Marcel moved along the sofa and put out his hand towards her. 'No, don't do that. It gives us a chance to talk…get to know each other, doesn't it? We're always rushing around when we're at the hospital.'

Debbie took a deep breath. It was so wonderful to be here in this peaceful house with a man who was becoming very important to her—too important, if she was honest with herself. He was sitting much closer to her now, his hand resting lightly on the back of the sofa behind her. So far she'd managed to hold her emotions in check. But, then, so far nothing had happened between them. And nothing of significance ever would if she could convince herself that she simply enjoyed counting Marcel amongst her friends.

She looked across at him now, quelling the mounting excitement at being so close to him.

'I feel I'm beginning to get to know you already, Marcel. I have to say, I found you a bit…how shall I put this?…difficult to work with on your first day in charge of Urgences. You seemed impossible to please.'

'And were you trying to please me?'

She suppressed a shiver at the intimate nuances in his deep sexy voice. Oh, this was so wicked, actually flirting with a man again! Dangerous, but delicious. But

46

being absolutely sure of how far she would go, she
knew she could handle her emotions, didn't she?

She was about to find out. 'Maybe I was trying to
please you…maybe I wasn't. I just thought you were a
bit of a tyrant.'

Marcel exploded with laughter. It was a rich dark
sound that reverberated around the high-ceilinged room.

'What's so funny?'

'You are, Debbie. Thinking of me as a tyrant. Well,
at least my plan worked.'

'Ah, so you were putting on an act?'

'Believe me, I was playing to the gallery that day! I
always do that when I take over a department. Show
the staff who's boss so that they know what to expect
if they're ever tempted to step out of line. When I became medical director of Urgences in my hospital in
Paris, I did exactly the same. And it meant I was rarely
disappointed in my staff. I had a brilliant team. I never
thought I would ever leave them.'

'What made you leave Paris?'

His enthusiastic expression changed as his face
clouded over. 'After my divorce I wanted a complete
break. Everywhere in Paris I was reminded of the happy
times Lisa and I had enjoyed together before…' He
broke off.

Debbie reached out and touched the side of his cheek.
He put his hand against hers and held it there for a few
seconds before placing her hand to his lips. She could
feel the warmth of his lips as gently he kissed the back
of her hand before releasing it and looking into her eyes.

'Were you very much in love?' Debbie asked gently,
trying not to show the emotions he'd aroused by the
touch of his lips.

He nodded. 'I worshipped Lisa…until I discovered

that the goddess I'd placed on a pedestal wasn't to be trusted. But you don't want to hear all this. You've had problems of your own so…'

'Please, go on.'

He leaned back against the sofa and closed his eyes as if to imagine more clearly the day when his illusions had been completely shattered.

'Lisa was a talented artist—still is a talented artist—but I prefer to think of her in the past tense. Hopefully, we will never meet again. She came out to Paris after she'd graduated from art school in England. When I first met her she had a small two-room apartment in Montmartre. One room was her studio, one her bedroom. We had a whirlwind romance and married after a few months.'

'It must have been very romantic.'

He opened his eyes, still looking up at the ceiling. 'It was.'

Debbie tried to quell the feeling of jealousy at the thought of Marcel having a romantic past. It was a stupid emotion she was feeling, completely irrational.

'Lisa kept on her apartment after we were married. She told me her father gave her a generous allowance. Every day she used to go off to Montmartre, ostensibly to paint. Looking back, I should have checked out what was happening but I was hopelessly in love with her and didn't question her fidelity. I was also terribly busy at the hospital.'

'Did you go to see her working in her studio?'

He shook his head. 'I couldn't understand why she asked me not to arrive without phoning first. And she actively discouraged me from visiting her during the time she was there. She said it would interrupt her creative flow…and I believed her.'

'So what actually did Lisa…?'

'She was entertaining her lover…or rather lovers. I believe she had at least two during the two years we were married.'

Debbie drew in her breath. 'How did you find out?'

'I was asked to take over from a professor of surgery at a residential conference on the outskirts of Paris. The professor had suffered a heart attack and I got an urgent call, asking me if I could take over immediately. I phoned Lisa at the studio but her phone was switched off. I decided to drive out to see her on my way to the conference. I parked in a little side street close to the apartment and…'

He stood up as his voice threatened to become too faint to continue. Walking over to the window, he looked out over the dark, brooding sea, the white caps of the waves illuminated by the lights from the shore. He realised he'd never told anybody the awful details of the day his dreams had been shattered. He'd kept it bottled up inside himself, saying that he couldn't bear to dwell on it. But Debbie was having such a calming effect on him he wanted to continue.

His natural instinct was to trust her not to repeat the story among his colleagues, but he knew he could never trust any woman ever again. He'd felt he could trust Lisa and look how wrong he'd been! The little voice of caution was telling him to be careful.

He turned round and walked back towards Debbie, taking strength from the concerned, sympathetic expression in her beautiful eyes. Surely he couldn't be wrong in wanting to take her into his confidence? Yes, he wanted to tell Debbie the whole story.

He took a deep breath. 'The studio door was open. I walked through and knocked on the door of her bedroom. After a few seconds a man opened the door, leaving it slightly ajar so he could peep out. But through the narrow gap I could see my wife reclining on the bed in a…very provocative pose.'

The dreadful memories were too poignant. He cleared his throat before continuing. 'I'll make it brief,' he said hoarsely. 'It transpired that her lover had expected me to be the delivery boy from the nearby wine bar bringing their order, otherwise he wouldn't have opened the door.'

Marcel took a deep breath. 'I'm glad he did open the door.'

'You're glad?'

'I'm glad now! It's always best to know the truth. But at the time I was furious. I forced my way in, intending to beat the pulp out of the man. My wife screamed at me to stop. Her lover didn't know she was married. He meant nothing to her and…'

Marcel put his head in his hands, breathing deeply with a loud rasping sound. Debbie waited for him to continue, not daring to stem the flow of his heartbreaking revelations. When he finally resumed his story he seemed calmer, more in control. He raised his head and looked directly at her.

'It was at that point I realised I'd never really known my wife. My sanity returned and I found I could review the situation realistically. Without a doubt it was over between us. I told Lisa I never wanted to see her again. She was still pleading with me as I walked out of her life. As soon as I could, I contacted my lawyer and instructed him to begin divorce proceedings.'

He sank down on the sofa beside her. 'I've never told anyone the whole painful story so I'd appreciate it if you keep it to yourself.'

'That goes without saying. I'm exactly the same about not wanting everyone to pity me. When I found out that Paul was deceiving me I contacted my solicitor and left everything to him. The big problem was how to explain to my two-year-old daughter.'

'Yes, it must be difficult when you have a child.' He leaned against the cushions, one arm gently resting on the back of the sofa behind her.

'Difficult and yet…' He paused. 'And yet I regret not being able to have a family. Coming from a large, warm family myself, I always intended to have children…but now I've accepted that it won't happen.'

'Why won't it happen?'

He looked surprised that she needed to ask. 'Because I'll never marry again.'

'Neither will I,' Debbie said firmly. She hesitated. 'But I can't stop wanting another child. I tell myself it's simply my hormones, my biological clock ticking away, but I can't stop that deep yearning inside me. I know I'd love to have another child.'

'Would you?'

His expressive voice was husky, full of sympathy but infinitely sexy as he turned towards her, putting both hands on the sides of her arms and drawing her closer until he was holding her in a gentle embrace, looking down at her with an expression of deep tenderness.

For one brief mad moment she thought how wonderful it would be to have a baby with this perfect hunk of a man! She knew he would be tantalisingly virile, impossible to resist… What was she thinking? She must never get herself into a situation where she couldn't resist a man, however desirable he might seem at the time. She was in charge of her emotions and wouldn't let herself get carried away with wild fantasies. Decisively, she eased herself away from Marcel.

He smiled. 'I'm sorry. I was only trying to be sympathetic.'

She looked across at him. 'I'm just not used to being alone with a man, that's all. It's been so long since I felt a man's arms round me and…actually, I was enjoying it too much,' she finished in a breathless rush.

'Too much? What do you mean?'

'I don't intend to ever get myself in a position where I'm not in charge again. Because losing yourself to a person means that…'

She broke off, unable to control her turbulent emotions. Unable to prevent herself, she moved towards him and touched his face, looking into his eyes and wanting to drown herself in all the tenderness she could see there.

'Marcel…would you just hold me like that again?' she whispered.

She didn't care if she was making a complete fool of herself. She simply wanted to experience the excitement of being in Marcel's arms, but only briefly and it wouldn't mean anything to either of them.

Gently he drew her into his embrace again. Only this time his arms were firmly around her. He looked down at her questioningly. She returned his gaze, her lips parted in hopeful anticipation, her mind completely closed to all warning signals from her conscience. She was flirting, tempting him, positively longing for what might happen.

He lowered his head towards her, she closed her eyes as his lips began to tease hers. She knew she couldn't escape her desire for him to kiss her. But still his lips only teased her. She pressed herself harder against his strong muscular chest as she felt his mouth steady on hers. His kiss deepened and she could feel she was losing all control of the situation. She wanted more, much more…but she didn't want the regrets that would come if she allowed herself to follow her heart.

With a swift determined move she pulled herself away and leaned back against the cushions, cautiously looking across at Marcel.

'You temptress!' he said in a husky voice. 'You were irresistible, Debbie.'

'I never intended to…'

'I know. We both understand each other, don't we? We're both trying to come to terms with life after divorce and the fact that we'll never commit ourselves again. But it's possible to have a little fun without being too serious about it, don't you think?'

Debbie smiled. 'It depends what you mean by fun. The trouble with me having fun is that I find it hard to stop.'

Marcel laughed. 'That sounds promising!'

Debbie laughed with him. So far so good! They'd managed to keep a light-hearted ambience and dismissed any suspicion that their deeply moving kiss had meant anything. Because it hadn't, had it? Not much!

'But I'm completely determined not to have another serious relationship,' Debbie said firmly.

'So am I!'

Their eyes met. Debbie had no idea what Marcel was thinking but she was already weighing up the possibilities of a light-hearted, no-strings romance.

'But not having a serious relationship means that I've got to come to terms with never having another baby,' Debbie said wistfully. 'You've managed to do that, haven't you?'

'Not really. What I say about accepting it and how I feel about the situation are two completely different ideas. If there was some way that—'

He broke off as the sound of the door chimes echoed through the room. 'That must be your driver.'

He stood up, putting out both hands to draw her to her feet. For a moment he held her in a loose embrace, before his lips came down on hers. She surrendered herself to the deliciously erotic vibes that were running through her body as their lips blended sensually together.

The doorbell chimed again. Debbie drew herself away and looked up into Marcel's eyes.

'Thank you for a wonderful evening, Marcel.'

'You must come here again…let's make it soon.'

She felt a shiver of sensual anticipation running down her spine. 'I'd like that very much.'

The small nagging voice of reason was trying to get through to her confused brain. 'I…er…I'll have to check my diary.'

Marcel grinned. 'Ah, yes, and then you'll have to find a babysitter and all the other excuses you like trotting out.'

She smiled. 'Am I so transparent?'

'You certainly are. But I understand where you're coming from and I respect you for it.'

He put a hand in the small of her back and led her out into the hall, before opening the door to Jérome.

Jérome began by apologising for keeping Debbie waiting. The spare tyre had also had a puncture, which his uncle had meant to ask him to repair but had forgotten to, and so…

Debbie found she wasn't really listening. She was simply wishing she could stay longer with Marcel, yet knowing that she would be treading on dangerous ground if…and when…she returned here.

Marcel watched the car driving out on to the main road before closing the door. He leaned against it and closed his eyes. What an evening this had been. Especially the final part where he'd been alone with Debbie. Ah, Debbie, the beautiful woman he'd been attracted to the first time he'd seen her. But that was his problem. Making instant judgements about someone. Not stopping to think where it might lead if he let himself get carried away…as he had done with Lisa, who'd been nothing like he'd first imagined.

But if he kept his feelings towards Debbie lighthearted and easygoing, no harm would come of it to either of them.

He began to move through the ground floor of the house, switching off lights, leaving the party clutter for his admirable *femme de ménage* to sort out when she came in to clean in the morning. Upstairs, he showered before lying down between the cool sheets, his thoughts still on Debbie. He couldn't stop thinking about her!

And even as he tried to get her out of his mind so he could go to sleep, the thought came to him that they could solve a great dilemma between them. Debbie wanted another baby. He'd tried to convince himself that he would be content not to father a child, but deep down the longing was still there. So if they both wanted a child and yet they didn't want a committed relationship, would it be possible for them to make a baby without becoming emotionally involved?

It would be fun trying! No, he told himself. With that sort of attitude he was doomed to failure. He had to look upon it in a medical way, as a clinical exercise so that their emotions remained under control. And they would have to agree that after the baby was conceived they would draw up a plan that made it quite clear where the boundaries of their relationship lay.

It would be important that the needs of the child were put first. Good parenting, even though the parents weren't committed to each other, was of paramount importance.

He ran his fingers through his hair as he realised the idea was infinitely too complicated. *Mon Dieu!* It would be impossible to take Debbie to bed and keep his true emotions under control! Just thinking about it was making him feel that if she were here with him now… No, he must stop that dangerous train of thought!

And what would Debbie think about all this? She would never agree. She would think he was mad. He'd better try to put it right out of his mind and get some sleep.

Debbie unlocked her front door. The house was aglow with lights but that was only Francoise making sure she wouldn't have to come back to a dark, unwelcoming house. What a treasure she was, Debbie thought as she went around switching off all the lights except those in the hall, on the stairs and in the kitchen. In the kitchen she opened the fridge and took out a carton of orange juice before sitting down at the table. Usually, at the end of the day she went straight up to her room and fell asleep almost as soon as her head touched the pillow.

She knew it was going to be difficult to stop thinking about the events of tonight. The party. Meeting up with her colleagues in a social situation which hadn't proved to be at all difficult, even though she'd been secretly dreading it. She'd now crossed the threshold and become a member of the post-divorce survivors' club! But the end of the evening, being alone with Marcel had been… She took a drink of her juice as she felt a frisson of excitement running through her.

Being alone with Marcel had been wonderful! Just having him all to herself, hearing the sad tale of his own disastrous marriage—something akin to her own. But she wasn't going to dwell on that tonight, not when she felt so fired up with excitement, so looking forward to the future again. And that was something she hadn't done for a long time! One day at a time had been her philosophy for so long. But, although the future stretched ahead of her in an exciting sort of way, she knew she could be heading for disaster if she allowed herself to make the same mistake again.

She mustn't allow herself to fall in love with Marcel! She must fight these strong feelings of attraction. She remembered how she'd looked across the sofa at him when they'd been discussing how they both wanted a child and… She swallowed hard. A child, a baby. She'd love another baby and as she'd looked at Marcel she'd allowed herself to fantasise about how marvellous it would be if he was the father of her baby!

She closed her eyes and for a few seconds let herself dwell on the idea. He would make the perfect father of her baby, quite apart from the fact that the act of conception would be… She shivered as she felt a deep erotic longing to be in Marcel's arms at this very moment! No, she had to stop wishing for the moon. Because if the dream of having Marcel as her baby's father came true—which it couldn't possibly, but if by some stretch of the imagination it did come true!—that would mean commitment, and neither of them wanted that.

She simply wanted a child who would be loved by her and its father for the whole of its life. Her own parents had managed to defy convention and make it work so that she'd always felt loved and wanted. So it could work if...

'I thought I heard you come in, Debbie.' Francoise walked into the kitchen, wearing the old dressing-gown she kept at the house for the times she stayed over. 'You look happy, so it was obviously a good evening.'

Debbie looked up, trying to come down to earth and think clearly again. 'Yes, it was a lovely party.'

'I hope Jérome's puncture didn't spoil the end of it for you.'

'No, no, it...' Debbie took a deep breath as she realised her voice was going all dreamy again. Get a grip, woman! 'Jérome got there as soon as he could and he's an excellent driver. I always feel so safe with him.'

Francoise smiled. 'Good. I'm glad all went well.'

'How was Emma?'

'Fine, she's a little angel! Would you like me to make you some hot chocolate?'

'*Non, merci*, Francoise. I'd better get some sleep. Busy day tomorrow—or rather today! Thanks for looking after Emma. I must go to bed now.'

She stood up and took her glass over to the sink, staring out dreamily at the moonlit garden before turning round and heading for the stairs. '*A demain*. I'll see you in the morning...'

Meeting up with Marcel the next morning in Urgences was a strange experience for Debbie. Standing next to him, studying the X-rays of a badly smashed leg, she was trying very hard to return to her former, professional, unemotional self. But it wasn't easy.

Think of the patient, she told herself. Remember the patient is going through a life-shattering experience and he needs all your sympathy. Marcel doesn't need anything from you except your professional judgement.

Marcel was pointing out the most badly injured area of the leg. 'This section will need pinning. Will you alert the orthopaedics team that early surgery is advisable—as in *aussi vite que possible*? As quickly as possible?'

Debbie nodded as she heard the urgent tone of Marcel's voice. She'd learned that he couldn't stand inefficiency and found it difficult to control his impatience.

'I'll see to it right away, Marcel,' she told him.

He smiled down at her and for an instant she basked in the warmth of his genuine smile before she moved away to set the wheels in motion for an early operation on their patient.

'Marcel! *Venez ici, immediatement, s'il vous plaît!*' Sister Marie's usually calm voice held a hint of panic as she got Marcel to follow her out of the cubicle to deal with the latest emergency.

It took only minutes for Debbie to alert the orthopaedic team and reassure her patient that he would be taken to Theatre for expert attention as soon as possible. Her patient, a holidaymaker from England, had been given painkillers but he was still in a highly distressed state after falling down a cliff higher up the coast.

'You're in good hands,' she told her patient gently. 'The orthopaedic team is excellent. The consultant will be here in a couple of minutes to explain what he's going to do and then—'

'Has anybody phoned my wife? I lost my mobile up there on the cliffs and—'

'I called her as soon as you came in. She's on her way. Ah, here's the orthopaedic consultant. Would you like me to act as interpreter or—?'

'Thank you, Doctor,' Fabien Arnaud said. 'I speak English to my patient. No problem. Besides, Marcel is asking for you to help him with this newly arrived emergency people.'

Debbie smiled down at her patient and squeezed his hand. 'I'll see you later, Mike.'

For a moment her patient clung to her hand before letting her go with a quiet, 'Thank you, Doctor.'

Marcel was in the treatment room, bending over an apparently lifeless patient, connected to resuscitation apparatus. Two members of the cardiac team were at the other side of the bed, trying desperately to restart the man's heart.

Marcel looked up as she went in, and she saw the desperation and frustration in his eyes.

'Take care of the boy and his mother,' he said quietly, his disconsolate voice showing how this difficult case was affecting him. 'My patient here swam out to save his son who'd got into difficulty in the waves. The boy was revived by the ambulance crew but...'

He raised his hands in a typically Gallic gesture, denoting his despair at the futility of trying to revive their patient who'd reacted as any devoted father would have when he'd realised his son was in danger.

Marcel turned back to his lifeless patient and looked across at the cardiac team. 'Let's try one more time.'

From the looks on the two doctors' faces it was obvious they felt they'd reached the end of all their resuscitation possibilities, but they complied with Marcel's instructions.

Debbie moved across the room to the couch where a

small boy of about eight was propped up against a pillow. His eyes widened with alarm as Debbie approached.

'*Mon père? Papa?* How is he?'

Debbie made an instant decision to take the boy into another cubicle. The chances of resuscitating the boy's father were extremely remote and she didn't want the boy to be there when the team decided they couldn't do any more.

Quietly she asked the boy his name.

'*Je m'appelle* Pierre.'

'*Je m'appelle* Debbie.'

'*Et mon papa*, Debbie…?'

'The doctors are doing everything they can, Pierre, but they need to be alone with your papa for the moment. So I'm going to take you to another cubicle so I can give you more attention.'

Quickly she called a porter so that they could move, and accompanied the boy to a nearby cubicle.

Carefully she began to check if Pierre had suffered any injuries. The boy lay still, his eyes staring up at the ceiling as she made a thorough examination.

There was a deep gash in his arm where the waves had buffeted him against some rocks.

'I'm going to put some stitches in your arm, Pierre,' she said gently. 'This cut will heal more easily if I do that so I'm going to make your arm feel cold around that area so that—'

'Is my papa going to die?' the boy whispered.

Debbie swallowed hard as she looked down at the frightened child. The boy was eight. She must answer as truthfully as she could. Thank goodness she had no problem with her French, she thought as she carefully answered the difficult question.

'Your father was very ill when the paramedics got him out of the sea. They were able to save you because you hadn't swallowed as much water as your papa. We are still hoping that we can save him.'

There was a loud scream from the outer reception area. 'No, he can't be dead. I won't believe it. I won't! What about my boy? Where's Pierre?'

The boy's eyes registered panic. He pulled himself up and grabbed hold of Debbie's white coat. 'That's my mother's voice. What did she say out there? She will be so cross with me for swimming too far out. She told me to—'

A woman rushed inside their cubicle and leaned over the boy, putting her arms around him.

'Pierre. Oh, my precious boy! You're alive! But your papa…'

The grieving mother stopped as she realised she had to become strong again for the sake of her son.

Debbie put her arm around the mother's trembling shoulders. The woman raised her tear-streaked face to her. 'Does my boy know that…?'

'You're going to tell me that Papa has died, aren't you, Maman?' Pierre said quietly.

For a moment he remained solemn and in control of himself, looking very grown-up. Then his little face crumpled and he clung to his mother. 'I'm sorry I swam too far out. I'm sorry Papa swam out to get me. I'm sorry…'

'You're a good boy, Pierre,' his mother said softly. 'I might have lost you. Be a brave boy now. Papa would want you to be brave.'

'I'm going to be brave.' Pierre looked up at Debbie. 'Do you want to stitch my cut now, Debbie?'

Debbie swallowed the lump in her throat as she pre-

pared the local anaesthetic. Poor child, having to come
to terms with the death of his father. He was being the
big brave boy at the moment, but as she stitched up the
long cut in his arm she was planning her next move in
caring for him. She would admit him to one of the preliminary care units and have him monitored by one of
the specialist care nurses throughout the forty-eight
hours of his stay.

Pierre's mother had been joined by her sister, an
older, very capable woman, who had arrived to give
moral support. Debbie was relieved that the grieving
woman wasn't alone as she went away to cope with the
necessary formalities that followed the death of a patient.

As Debbie finished writing out a report of the patients
she'd cared for during the day, her usual sense of
achievement was tinged with sadness over the death of
Pierre's father. She sat back against her chair and stared
at the computer screen for a moment as she dealt with
the surge of emotion you weren't supposed to allow
yourself to dwell on if you were going to be an objective, composed doctor.

'I thought I'd find you here, Debbie.'

She looked up as Marcel walked in. 'I'm technically
off duty but I needed to finish this report before I go.
Pierre's father was your patient but I need to mention
the effect his death had on the boy. I want to make sure
that the staff in the preliminary unit are going to spend
a lot of time with him. For one thing, he feels guilty
that he was the one who caused his father to swim out.
And guilt when you're only eight years old is difficult
to handle.'

Marcel eased himself down onto the corner of her

desk. 'Guilt at any age is difficult to handle. Don't worry, he's being carefully monitored and counselled by paediatric specialists. At least he's physically fit and he has a beautiful piece of embroidery on his arm.'

Debbie smiled as she felt her spirits lifting again.

'That's better, Debbie! It's good to see a smile on your face. I knew you'd be sad about losing a patient. So am I because I was still hoping for a miracle even at the very end when the others had given up.'

He shrugged his broad shoulders. 'But I'm always an optimist. I hate defeat.'

He leaned across the desk and put one finger under her chin, tilting it up towards him. 'So, as we've both been defeated today, I thought we needed cheering up. Why don't you come back to my place for supper tonight? You can phone that wonderful lady who takes care of your daughter when you're not there and tell her you—'

'I can't!' The touch of Marcel's finger on her face had been deliciously sensual. She couldn't cope with anything more...at the moment.

He gave a deep sigh. 'Why did I know that would be your answer?'

'I can't leave Emma two nights in succession, can I?'

He gave her a wicked grin. 'Are you asking me or telling me?'

'Well, I'm simply saying that, as a mother, I ought to—'

'Ah, the guilt thing!' He grinned. 'Are you worrying that your daughter will suffer if you're not with her tonight or...?'

'Tonight!' she echoed. 'I'm not planning to stay the night!'

Marcel stood up and came around the back of her

chair, placing an arm around her shoulders. 'Who said anything about staying the night?' he said in a soft, seductive voice.

'I got confused with my French,' she countered.

He drew her to her feet so that she was effectively in his embrace as she looked up at him. 'Then let's speak English this evening when you come for supper.'

She could feel her heart beating loudly and she was sure that Marcel would be able to feel the thumping as he held her against his thin cotton shirt.

'I'd like to come to supper but—'

'Then you must come! Your daughter will enjoy another evening of being spoilt and the lady who helps you...'

'Francoise.'

'Francoise will be overjoyed to have her little treasure all to herself again. Make the call now.'

Debbie smiled as she tried to ignore the boring voice of reason that was nagging her. 'I think you just talked me into it.'

She felt her heart churning with excitement as she picked up the phone. What was she letting herself in for?

'Francoise? *C'est* Debbie. *Est-ce-que c'est possible que...* Do you think you could possibly...?'

CHAPTER FOUR

DEBBIE looked across the kitchen table at Marcel. 'Where did you learn to cook like this?'

Marcel smiled as he placed the casserole of *poulet grand-mère* in front of her so she could help herself.

'I learned to cook at home in Paris. My mother was a paediatrician in charge of the medical care of the schoolchildren in a large arrondissement in Paris. She worked extremely hard and she was often late home. We all learned to cook so that most of the dinner would be ready by the time she got home. My father was a surgeon so he often didn't arrive until late.'

'Did you have any domestic help?'

'There was a *femme de ménage* who came in a couple of days a week to clean. Our grandmother lived with us and she ensured that the domestic work was organised. She also taught all of us to cook from the moment we could stir a spoon in a bowl so that we could help her in the evenings when she was tired.'

'How many brothers and sisters did you have?'

'I was the youngest of three boys and two girls.'

Debbie sighed. 'Sounds idyllic!'

Marcel laughed. 'It was far from idyllic at times! But it's the sort of family life I always wanted for myself if…' His voice trailed away.

'Me, too,' Debbie said quietly, laying down her fork. 'I was an only child and I intended to have lots of children. But Paul put paid to that.'

'Paul was your husband?'

Debbie nodded. 'For three years. When Emma was two I discovered he'd had a series of affairs—two or three, actually. I never did find out how many. When I accidentally overheard one of the nurses talking to a colleague about the affair going on between my husband and a young nurse, that was when my illusions about Paul were shattered. It was only a matter of time before various colleagues enlightened me after I'd told them I was planning to divorce him.'

'Same scenario as my own disastrous marriage,' Marcel commented in a sympathetic voice. 'Any regrets now?'

'Only that I married the wrong man and didn't get the family I wanted,' she said quietly. 'I adore my wonderful daughter but I never intended her to be an only child.'

'I can imagine how you feel.'

He hesitated. Now wasn't the time to broach the subject that had been uppermost in his mind since they'd been alone together after his party. Perhaps later…or perhaps not! Looking across the table at his lovely companion, he didn't want anything to spoil the evening. When they'd spent more time together he would be able to evaluate the possibilities of his mad idea.

He deliberately steered the conversation onto neutral subjects, so that they were soon discussing books they'd recently read, music they liked to listen to, places they'd travelled to or intended to go to at some time in the future.

'At least, with only one child it will be easier for me to travel,' Debbie said. 'My mother took me everywhere with her when I was small. She always had a busy schedule but she made time for me, somehow fitting in her surgical training and working her way up to becoming a consultant surgeon. And she always made sure the two of us had great holidays together.'

'So where was your father?' Marcel asked, as he placed fruit and cheese on the table.

'Ah, that's a long story.' Debbie picked up an apple and began to peel it as she started to explain her background. 'You see, my parents never married. They met in London when my French surgeon father came over to the medical school where my mother was a final-year student. They had a whirlwind romance lasting several months during which my father used to come over to London as often as he could get away from his work in Paris.'

'Sounds very romantic.'

'My father told me it was. My mother rarely spoke about it, only to tell me that just after she'd finished her final exams she discovered she was pregnant. My father wanted them to get married. My mother said she didn't want the commitment of marriage. She wanted to keep her independence. They discussed what was best for the baby she was carrying and my father insisted that his child should know he was the father.'

'Very wise,' Marcel commented, as he felt his interest growing in the details of Debbie's background. 'Did your father make any other stipulations?'

'Oh, Mum said they both had a rational discussion about what was going to happen in the future. My father was to be part of my life but at a distance. In other words, the emotional bond he'd shared with my mother was to end.'

'Sounds complicated.'

'Oh, it wasn't! I had a great childhood. My father was always there when I needed him. I didn't feel I missed out on anything—except having brothers and sisters. After my father married and had two daughters, I enjoyed being with them when I went over to Paris. But they were much younger than me. It's only in recent years that my stepsisters and I have grown closer.'

'Seems like your parents found the perfect solution,' Marcel said, deciding that he would, after all, be able to put forward his idea. Maybe his plan wasn't as mad as he'd first feared.

'And what sort of relationship do your parents enjoy now?'

Debbie hesitated before she could find her voice again. It still hurt. 'My mother died in a skiing accident when I was at medical school.'

'I'm so sorry. I wouldn't have asked if…'

'That's OK. I should be over it by now, but my mother had been the centre of my life while I was growing up and…and I found it hard to come to terms with. That's when my father asked me to go and live with his family in Paris. I regarded it as my home during my holidays from medical school, but after I qualified I found my own place in London.'

He stood up. 'Let's have our coffee in the sitting room. You go through, Debbie. I'll bring the cafetière as soon as it's ready.'

'Let me help with the dishes…'

'That's OK. I'll stack the dishwasher later. Go and make yourself comfortable.'

He switched on the coffee-grinder and conversation was no longer possible. Debbie got the impression she wasn't wanted in the kitchen any more. Marcel appeared deep in thought as he set out crockery on a tray. She made her way to the sitting room and walked over to admire the view over the sea as she had done the previous evening.

As Marcel spooned the ground coffee beans into the cafetière he found it hard to contain his mounting excitement. Debbie's parents had made it work. They'd successfully had a child together who hadn't suffered because they hadn't been committed to each other. So it could be possible. But they would both have to agree.

Debbie turned round from the window as she heard Marcel arriving with the coffee.

'Such a beautiful view! I love watching the lights on the ships moored close to the shore.'

Marcel placed the tray on a small table beside the sofa before walking over to join Debbie at the window. As casually as possible, he put an arm around her shoulders, drawing her gently against him. He waited to feel her body stiffen with rejection but instead she seemed to be relaxing.

'I often stand here in the evenings,' he began, his voice husky, feeling more than a little disturbed at their closeness to each other. 'Just watching the dark sea, occasionally following the path of an illuminated boat. It's a good way of winding down after a stressful day. It feels even better this evening.'

Debbie looked up at him, her eyes searching his expressive face. He was gazing down at her with real tenderness. She realised that she was longing for him to take her in his arms. One little kiss, that was all it would take to…

As he lowered his head and kissed her, oh, so gently on the lips it was almost as if he'd been reading her thoughts. She parted her lips to savour the moment, knowing that her feelings must have been blatantly obvious. But Marcel was already pulling himself away.

'Come and have some coffee.'

As Marcel took hold of Debbie's hand and led her

over to the sofa, he was thinking that he had to tread carefully this evening. If he was to put forward his plan for them to have a baby together, he must hold onto his emotions. Debbie would never agree if she thought he was angling for a permanent emotional bond between them.

He hadn't been able to resist her just now, but he would have to learn how to be more emotionally objective if the plan was to succeed. She'd looked so beguiling as she'd gazed up at him. He loved her clear blue eyes, the gentle curve of her inviting mouth. Simply looking at her when they were alone turned him on.

Debbie sank down against the cushions. On the one hand she was relieved that their kiss had been a spur-of-the-moment action, but on the other hand she knew that she'd wanted more. Her whole body was crying out to be loved by Marcel. She took a couple of deep breaths to calm herself.

Marcel was placing a small porcelain coffee cup on the table beside her. He sat down at the other end of the sofa. They looked at each other over the expanse of cushions stacked between them.

Marcel cleared his throat. 'I'm deliberately sitting at this end of the sofa because I've got a plan to put forward to you and I want to be totally objective about it… No, don't look so worried. I simply want to… Oh, this is going to be so difficult to put into words…'

'Sounds intriguing.' Her heart began to beat faster.

'We've talked before about the fact that we'd both love to have a child but don't want to have a committed relationship.'

'We have.' Her heart was absolutely thumping now. Was Marcel going to suggest that they come to some arrangement between them? The thought of Marcel being the father of her child was a magic idea. She could see him in her mind's eye holding their baby, sitting beside her bedside, holding her hand…

She checked her thoughts. The scenario she'd just imagined could never happen…or could it?

'I think I know what you're going to say,' she blurted out, unable to contain herself.

'You do?' He seemed relieved.

'Is it something to do with what I was telling you earlier…about me having a father figure in my life who didn't live with my mother?'

Marcel smiled. 'It could be just that. And as we're speaking English, you've got the advantage over me. So why don't you tell me what you think my plan might be?'

She moved into the centre of the sofa. Marcel moved closer and casually put his arm along the back of the sofa. He felt a sense of relief flooding through him. Maybe Debbie was already thinking along the same lines.

'I think because we both want a baby…' Debbie began carefully. 'Because it's what we both want, you're wondering if it wouldn't be possible to produce one between us.'

'That sounds very cold and clinical but…'

'Oh, but it would have to be!'

Even as she said that, Debbie knew it would be impossible to remain totally detached during the act of conception. If one small kiss threw her emotions into turmoil, what would a long session in bed with Marcel do to her?

'I think we would find it extremely difficult to remain emotionally detached during the act of conception,'

Marcel said. 'Let's look at the facts. We both want a baby but we don't want commitment. We both want the baby to have a father figure who's there for our baby when needed. Am I correct?'

Debbie nodded. 'That's about the sum of it.'

Marcel stood up and began pacing the room. 'Your parents achieved that and you had a happy childhood. They were able to live independent lives. I don't think the mood they were in during the act of conception made any difference whatsoever. They were able to conceive in the normal way and then continue to remain uncommitted to each other while being committed to the child.'

He was standing by the window again, one hand on the window-sill, turning sideways to look at Debbie.

Debbie stood up and joined him at the window, deliberately standing a few paces away as she tried to remain totally objective.

'The two situations are different. My parents were having a whirlwind romance when I was conceived. I don't suppose they were planning to have a baby. I don't imagine either of them was looking too far into the future. But we know exactly what we want in our future lives, don't we?'

Marcel drew closer and placed his hands on her shoulders. 'Do we?' he said softly.

He knew he should be trying to make sure their discussion continued in an emotionally detached manner, but it was impossible for him to remain cold and clinical when he was anywhere near Debbie.

Debbie was finding the touch of his hands undermining her resolve. She looked up into his eyes, unnerved even more by his expression of real tenderness. 'We both want a baby. We both want to be loving parents, committed to the baby but not to each other. And that's why we would have to be careful during the act of conception not to become too…er…too…'

Marcel gave her a rakish grin. 'Too what, Debbie?'

'Oh, Marcel, don't tease me! You know perfectly well what I mean.'

'Too loving towards each other?'

She swallowed hard. 'Something like that, only…'

'What you mean is that we mustn't fall in love,' he said breathily.

'Exactly!'

'Well, then, if I sign a paper to say I promise not to fall in love while I'm making you pregnant will you…?'

They were both laughing now as he drew her into his arms, nuzzling his lips against her hair.

Debbie was revelling in the feel of his arms around her. She loved the fact that the tension between them had eased. But as far as not falling in love with this wonderful man was concerned, she just knew it would be impossible. She'd fallen too far already.

'It's not going to work, is it?' she whispered.

'We'll make it work,' he said, his voice serious again. 'Because it's what we both want. And even if we do get carried away while we're making love…sorry… trying to conceive a child, we'll be able to come down to earth afterwards and go out into the real world as independent, uncommitted people. Don't you think?'

He was looking down at her with that same tender look that had taken away her resolve earlier. His question still hung in the air. She decided to treat herself to one small kiss again to see if she could remain emotionally detached. She raised her lips towards his.

He smiled as he brought his lips down on hers. His

kiss deepened. Debbie could feel her treacherous body responding. She'd already proved what she'd planned to find out. It would be impossible to make love with Marcel and remain detached. But Marcel thought there would be no problem if they were to lose themselves for a while…a heavenly time together it would be…and then simply walk away and continue with their everyday lives. But…

Her body was responding too much now but, oh, it was the most delicious feeling. She moulded herself against Marcel's strong, virile, muscular body. His hands were caressing her face, her neck, gently beginning to tease her breasts… She was beginning to lose control…

She pulled away, panting with suppressed frustration as she gazed up at him indecisively. More than anything else she wanted him to sweep her away to his bedroom where they would make wonderful love, and she wouldn't give any thought to the future.

Gently, he caressed the side of her cheek. 'We could always have a rehearsal, couldn't we?'

There was nothing she would have liked better…which was why she'd better call a halt now while she was still in control.

'Marcel, I'm still not sure it would work. Let me have some time to think about it.'

'Of course. Take all the time you need.'

'I'll phone for a taxi,' she said quickly, before she could change her mind. 'Jérome took me in this morning because my car's being serviced. I told him I'd get a taxi back when—'

'I'll drive you home.' His voice was masterful, serious, brooking no argument.

'There's no need, really.'

He ignored her protest. 'I'll get your jacket.'

They were both quiet in the car, each deep in their own thoughts. Marcel was disappointed that they hadn't resolved anything that evening, but he was still optimistic that Debbie would come round to his way of thinking. A child was what they both wanted. And even if they both got carried away at the conception—which they doubtless would!—they could try hard to redress the balance afterwards. Or could they?

Just sitting beside Debbie now, the intimate scent of her perfume teasing his nostrils, the close proximity of her sexy, alluring body... He checked his thoughts as he almost groaned aloud. Did she have any idea of the effect she was having on him? He was feeling decidedly uncomfortable as he tried to control his body, which was aching for fulfilment.

'Our house is around the next corner, at the end of the street through the village... Yes, there it is, the one with the lights on. Can't think why all the lights are on so late.'

As Marcel pulled the car into the drive, the door opened. Francoise stood framed in the doorway, peering out into the darkness.

'*C'est toi*, Debbie?'

'*Oui, c'est moi*, Francoise. *Qu'est-ce qu'il y a?*'

Debbie got out of the car. Marcel followed close behind her.

'It's Emma,' Francoise said in a worried tone. 'I was just going to phone you on your mobile but I couldn't leave her. She cut her leg on the corner of the kitchen cabinet and...'

Debbie and Marcel moved quickly into the house. Francoise continued to tell them the details as they hurried through into the kitchen.

'Just a few minutes ago Emma came downstairs and asked if she could have a hot chocolate drink. I said I would make it in a few minutes, as soon as the television programme ended. She went into the kitchen, climbed up to the cupboard, lost her balance and fell.'

'Mummy!' Emma was sitting on a chair, her bandaged leg stretched out across another chair. 'I'm sorry I climbed up. I was just trying to help Francoise and—'

'That's OK, darling. Let's take a look and see what's happened here.'

Debbie began unwrapping the bandage that Francoise had carefully applied. Francoise stood to one side, trembling with the shock of coping with an injured Emma.

Marcel leaned across to look at the wound. It was better than he'd feared, but it was deep enough to require suturing.

'I'll get my medical bag and we'll soon have this cut fixed,' Debbie said, moving swiftly out of the kitchen.

Marcel knelt down at the little girl's side while he held a section of the bandage over the cut to staunch the flow of blood.

'Could have been worse, Emma,' he said in a reassuring voice.

Emma regarded the unknown man solemnly. 'Who are you?'

'I'm Marcel. I work at the hospital with your mummy.'

'You speak good English.'

'Thank you.'

'But you're French really, aren't you?'

'I am indeed.'

'I thought so. I can always tell. French people speaking English make it sound funny.'

Marcel smiled as he thought what an engaging little girl Emma was. A pleasure to talk to.

'What do you mean?' he asked.

Emma grinned. 'Well, you know, like…' She exaggerated a French accent superimposed on an English phrase.

Marcel laughed. 'That was very good. Does that sound like me?'

'No, your English is quite good really.'

'Praise indeed! Ah, here's Mummy.'

As she came back into the kitchen Debbie witnessed the touching scene of Marcel getting to know Emma. She needn't have worried about leaving them together. The two of them were getting on like a house on fire.

Marcel leaned to one side so that Debbie could begin tending the wound. He removed the portion of bandage he'd been holding and they conferred.

'It needs a couple of stitches, maybe three, to hold the edges together,' Debbie said as she swabbed the site of the wound with antiseptic.

'Will it hurt when you stitch me, Mummy? You stitched my teddy bear and he didn't cry, but I think I might…'

Big tears loomed in Emma's eyes and began to spill down her pale cheeks. 'I'm trying to be brave but…'

'Would you like me to give you a magic numbing potion?' Marcel asked. 'You won't feel a thing after one tiny little prick from the needle at the end of my syringe.'

'Is it really magic?'

Debbie flashed him a grateful look. Dealing in a detached way with her own child was always stressful. She stepped aside so that Marcel could select a sterile syringe for the local anaesthetic from Debbie's bag.

'It's a kind of magic,' Marcel explained as he prepared the syringe. 'It's medicine really, but it works like magic. Now, this is the tiny prick you're going to feel. Imagine it's a fly that's settled on your leg and it's tickling you.'

Emma smiled. 'I felt it tickling me. Was that it?'

'That's it. All I've got to do now is pretend you're a teddy bear and sew you up in the bit that you can't feel any more.'

Watching Marcel expertly suturing Emma's cut, Debbie felt a lump in her throat. He was being so kind and caring with her daughter. He would make a wonderful father. And he actually wanted to father her child! What could be more fantastic? Except that the sort of contract she would want wouldn't be the cold clinical kind. The walk-away-afterwards-and-remain-detached kind.

She would want the whole works, the complete scenario, Marcel holding her hand when she went into labour, Marcel at the bedside, Marcel beside her all through the baby's childhood. So what was she going to do about it?

'There you go. Good as new!' Marcel stood back as if to admire his handiwork.

'Thank you, Marcel,' Debbie said.

Francoise came forward. She'd stopped trembling and was smiling with relief. 'I'm so glad you came home when you did, Debbie.' She turned to look at Marcel. 'And you're a doctor, too.'

'Marcel De Lange.' He shook hands with Francoise, who was clearly charmed to meet him.

'I'll make that drink of hot chocolate now for you, Emma,' Francoise said.

'No, I'll make it,' Debbie said. 'You must be tired, Francoise. Do you want to stay the night or…?'

'I'd better get home. I'm going on an early shopping trip tomorrow morning to Le Touquet with my sister.'

'You must let me drive you home, Francoise,' Marcel said.

'I only live at the end of the street,' Francoise said.

'It's on my way,' Marcel said. 'Goodnight, Emma. Goodnight, Debbie.' He smiled. 'You'd better stay with the patient so I'll see myself out.'

'Thanks for the stitching,' Emma said. 'I can't wait to show it to my friends at school.'

Marcel turned at the kitchen door. 'I'll see you tomorrow, Debbie.'

She smiled. Nobody looking at the two of them making their civilised goodbyes would guess that they'd just had a most important discussion that hadn't been resolved.

'Mummy, I don't think I want any hot chocolate now,' Emma said. 'I only asked for it so I could come downstairs for a while. Francoise is so kind. She always says yes when I want a drink. But what I really want now is to go to bed because I'm falling asleep.'

Debbie hoisted her daughter over her shoulder and carried her up the stairs. In a matter of minutes, as she sat at her daughter's bedside reading one of her favourite stories, she saw Emma's eyes drooping. Her breathing changed into the soft sounds of childish slumber.

Debbie put out the bedside light, leaving on the small night-light in the corner of the room before going along to the bathroom. She shed her clothes and climbed into the bath for a long soak. Although she was tired she knew that it would be difficult to sleep while her mind was so active with thoughts of Marcel's plan.

She poured more bath foam in and lay back amongst the bubbles. Mmm…this was blissful. It would be even more blissful if Marcel were here with her. This old bath was big enough for two. Now, wouldn't that be a wonderful experience, a sort of prelude to going to her bed and making love? No, making a baby would be the object of their love-making but it would still be an act of love, whatever she tried to call it.

She knew she wanted more than anything to make a baby with Marcel. The conception itself would be blissful! But it was the aftermath that was completely uncharted territory. How could she possibly walk away from Marcel when they'd made love together? Because it would be making love, on her part anyway. She couldn't speak for Marcel, but from the vibes he'd been putting out tonight she doubted that remaining cool and clinical would be uppermost in his mind.

There was no solution to that problem. Perhaps she should put off giving Marcel an answer for a few days. Yes, that's what she would do. A little procrastination never hurt anybody. Especially when the question under consideration was one of life-changing propensities.

Driving home, Marcel pulled to the side of the road and switched off the engine. His mind was in a whirl. He'd thought Debbie was about to agree to his idea, but then she'd got scared about it.

He looked out through the windscreen. There was a full moon tonight, the landscape lit up almost like daylight. At the bottom of the hill the sea sparkled with shafts of moonlight on the foam-flecked waves.

It hadn't helped that he'd frightened Debbie away by

coming on too strong. But it was so difficult to react in any other way when he found her so attractive, so vibrant, so sexy, so...

No, he told himself. He had to remain more detached next time. If there was a next time. She would probably give a resounding no to his plan and that would be the end of what had promised to be a beautiful friendship. Until Debbie gave him an answer he would remain friendly but would refrain from anything more. In fact, he wouldn't bring up the subject again until she did.

As he restarted the engine he prayed that Debbie wouldn't take too long deciding what she wanted to do.

CHAPTER FIVE

FOR the next few days, Debbie was surprised to find that Marcel didn't refer to their discussion about creating a baby together. Neither did he suggest they get together to review the situation. He was polite and professional when they worked together in the hospital but gave no hint of what had passed between them.

At least it gave her some more time to think about what she wanted to do. Perhaps he'd completely gone off the idea. He hadn't suggested they see each other in their off-duty time either. Perhaps, like her, he realised the baby plan would be an irrevocable and therefore dangerous step to take.

At the end of a week she decided that she would have to be the one to broach the subject, even though she knew that nothing had changed as far as she was concerned. She realised that she wouldn't be able to control her emotions during the act of conceiving a baby. And returning to a companiable friendship afterwards would be impossible. She didn't want to lose Marcel's friendship, so what was she to do?

As she walked across the main reception area of Urgences she decided she would have to bring up the subject today. It would have to be this evening because they were both on duty all day.

There was a lot of screaming going on from a patient who was being wheeled in. She hurried over to investigate. A middle-aged woman was clinging to her grey-haired husband's hand as he held onto the stretcher with the other. He was trying to comfort his wife but the screams were getting louder.

'I can't bear the pain… *Je ne peux plus supporter…* Oh, ooh…'

'*C'est ma femme Béatrice, docteur.* I brought her in as soon as I could,' the man said anxiously. 'She collapsed at home. Just lay there on the sofa, screaming. She's got this terrible pain in her stomach. It goes right through to her back.'

Debbie had instructed the porter who was wheeling the trolley to bring the patient into the treatment room. Together they heaved the exceptionally heavy woman onto the examination couch. The patient seemed to calm herself temporarily as she looked up at Debbie.

Debbie took a tissue and mopped her patient's brow. 'How old are you, Béatrice?' she asked quietly.

'*J'ai quarante sept ans*, forty-seven. *Mon Dieu*, it's coming again. That awful pain. I can't bear it. I can't… Oh, aagh…'

Debbie pulled back the blanket that was covering her patient. The woman had an excess of flesh all over her body but the abdomen was particularly distended. Debbie put her hand over the abdomen and felt the unmistakable rippling of a strong muscular contraction. The immediate diagnosis was obvious.

'When did you have your last period, Béatrice?' Debbie asked as the contraction died down.

'Oh, I don't know. Ages ago. I'm in the menopause, Doctor.'

Debbie knew her diagnosis was going to come as a shock! She prepared herself to be very gentle with her patient when she explained what was happening.

'I'm just going to examine you down below,' she said

as she manoeuvred her patient into a lithotomy position with her legs wide apart.

The worried husband turned white and said he didn't feel well. He was going to go outside for a cigarette but he would come back as soon as he felt better.

Debbie became aware that Marcel had come in and was now standing at the other side of the examination couch.

'It sounded like you might need some help,' he said. 'This looks to me as if we…'

Debbie raised her head from examining her patient.

'Imminent delivery,' she said quietly. 'Fully dilated cervix.'

Marcel was already scrubbing his hands at the sink.

'What are you doing?' Béatrice called out. 'What's the matter with me?'

'You're in labour, Béatrice,' Debbie said calmly, as she wheeled over the Entonox machine and adjusted the painkilling flow of gas and air through the mask. 'You're having a baby.'

'I can't be! I told you, I'm in the menopause. I'm a grandmother, for heaven's sake… Ooh, it's coming again, Doctor, Doctor…'

Béatrice grabbed Debbie's hand.

'Breathe into this mask, Béatrice. Deep breaths. That's the way. This will help the pain. You can hold it yourself like this…'

Marcel was now bending over the patient. Gowned and gloved, he was examining the birth canal. He looked up briefly at Debbie and nodded.

'Yes, cervix fully dilated. The head is now crowning. Don't let Béatrice push. Hold off…it's crucial to hold off until the head…'

He was quiet for a few seconds as he investigated further.

'The cord is round the baby's neck,' Marcel told Debbie in a calm voice that only she could hear. 'I'm going to unhook it… I'm nearly there… Yes! It's OK now. Béatrice can push on the next contraction.'

Debbie breathed a sigh of relief. The main danger was over. Bearing in mind that her patient was in her late forties, there could be further complications but the birth was going smoothly for the moment. As the tiny infant emerged, slipping easily into Marcel's hands, it gave a loud cry.

'Nothing wrong with baby's lungs,' Marcel said, as he cut the cord and wrapped the vociferous baby in a dressing towel. He looked across at Debbie. Their eyes met and locked in a long, meaningful gaze.

'It's a girl,' he said huskily. 'Béatrice has a perfect little baby girl. Isn't that wonderful?'

Debbie swallowed the lump in her throat. 'Yes, I agree.'

She knew without a shadow of a doubt that she had to go ahead with their plan. She desperately wanted to have a baby. She wanted to have Marcel's baby.

'You do? You agree to…?'

It was a poignant, momentous, private moment between the two of them. It was as if there was nobody else in the room. In that instant they'd both acknowledged that they wanted to have a baby together, whatever the problems that might lie ahead.

Marcel was holding the baby close as he moved towards her. Gently he put the child in Debbie's arms. It was as if they were signing the agreement, saying to each other, One day soon, we'll get together and…

Their hands briefly touched as she took the baby into

her arms, holding her close. She was quieter now, but her little fists were waving in the air. The whole of her tiny body was vibrant with life. Try as she may, Debbie couldn't stop a lone tear from trickling down her cheek, though whether it was from happiness or longing she couldn't imagine.

'When you've finished drooling over the baby,' Marcel whispered in English, 'you'd better see if Béatrice has recovered enough to hold her.'

Their patient was lying very still with her eyes closed. The gas and air she'd been breathing had made her drowsy and confused.

'Would you like to hold your baby girl, Béatrice?' Debbie asked.

The new mother opened her eyes to focus on the tiny infant in the doctor's arms. She felt very confused. There had been a lot of pain. She'd breathed in that gassy stuff and now she just wanted to sleep. Was that really her baby? She'd felt the other doctor poking around down there, but she hadn't believed it was happening to her. She would wake up soon and find it had all been a dream.

The door opened and in came Béatrice's husband.

'Mon Dieu! C'est pas possible! Le bébé…?'

Marcel sat the man down on a chair. His previous pallor had deepened and taken on a greenish shade.

'Yes, it's your baby,' Debbie said gently, as she helped Béatrice to hold the infant in her arms. 'You've got a perfect little girl.'

'Frédéric, come and have a look at our daughter,' Béatrice said weakly, as the memories of what the doctor had told her came flooding back. The doctor wouldn't make up a story like that, would she? 'She's a little miracle.'

The astounded husband put his arm round his wife's shoulders as he leaned down to kiss the tiny infant on the top of her downy head.

Marcel drew Debbie to one side. 'All babies are miracles,' he whispered softly. 'But it would be a miracle if you would take the first step. Did you really mean you…?'

Debbie looked up into his eyes. 'Yes. I agree,' she whispered. 'I made up my mind just now when I saw that darling little girl arriving. I want us to have a baby together. I want Emma to have a brother or sister. I don't know how it will work out in the future but…'

Marcel put one finger against her lips. 'Shh,' he murmured. 'We'll work it out together.'

Debbie nodded. 'Of course we will.' She turned to look at the happy new mother and father, now perfectly reconciled to the idea of becoming parents again. 'I'd better start the postnatal checks.'

'I've always wanted a girl. We've got a son of twenty-six and three grandsons,' Frédéric told Debbie proudly as she took the baby from Béatrice. 'So this little girl is going to make history in our family.'

'She's already made history by arriving unexpectedly like she did,' Béatrice said, running a hand through her damp, greying hair. 'I've no idea where she came from.'

Frédéric grinned. 'Oh, I have. It was after that party your sister gave when—'

'Frédéric! Don't embarrass me!' Béatrice giggled. 'What I mean is, I had no idea I was pregnant. It wasn't a bit like when I had Jean-Pierre, although it's so long ago I suppose I must have forgotten about it. What I do remember is that with Jean-Pierre I was in labour for…'

Debbie continued to check out the new baby as Béatrice reminisced with her husband. She was feeling elated at having made the momentous decision. She wasn't going to change her mind now.

A couple of nurses arrived from Obstetrics. Marcel had already contacted the consultant in charge of that department to give him a full report of the situation.

As soon as Béatrice and her family had been transferred, Debbie went along to her small office at the other end of Urgences. She needed to write a brief report and check her messages before she resumed work. The emergency area was relatively quiet. The staff were coping with the patients already there, and unless there was some major disaster the day would be routine.

She switched on the small electric hotplate in the corner of her office, put water and coffee in her little cafetière and settled down to deal with her messages while she waited for the coffee to brew.

'Do I smell coffee?' Marcel pushed open the door, walked in and sat down on the only other chair in the room.

Debbie smiled and swivelled her chair around from the computer. 'You must have the most amazing sense of smell if you can detect coffee from the emergency area.'

Marcel grinned. 'I saw you slipping away and I hoped you'd be switching on your high-tech coffee-machine.'

'You mean low-tech,' Debbie said as she rushed across to the ancient contraption, which had begun to boil over. 'I keep meaning to buy myself an electric kettle and some instant coffee.'

'In France?' Marcel look scandalised. 'Where do you think you are? England?'

Debbie laughed. 'No comment.'

She placed two small cups on the small table near the desk.

'Coffee's good,' Marcel remarked as he took a tentative sip. 'But I didn't come here only for a cup of coffee. I came to make sure that you really have agreed and won't change your mind.'

'No.'

'*Non?*'

'No, I won't change my mind. Yes, I've agreed…but we need to talk about…'

Marcel put down his coffee-cup. It rattled in the saucer as he thumped his hand on the edge of the desk.

'*Non*, the time for talking is over,' he said forcefully. 'We need to act now, before we think up any more reasons why we shouldn't go ahead. Let's be totally positive and objective about this. When we have achieved a pregnancy, then is the time to draw up rules about the baby's future. Better we get started, and the sooner the better! How about tonight, my place?'

Debbie swallowed hard. She'd only seen Marcel as forceful as this when he was working on a difficult emergency case. Being masterful, taking charge of a situation always suited him. So she would simply go along with what he suggested for the first part of their plan. But tonight?

'Tonight? I'm afraid tonight's out of the question.'

'Why? What excuse have you dreamed up now?'

'It's not an excuse! I need to make proper arrangements with Francoise. I'll have to make sure it's convenient for her to stay the night.'

'Francoise doesn't have to stay the night. I can drive you home afterwards.'

'But I thought it might be better if I stay the whole night.'

As soon as she'd said it, she knew it had been a mistake. It was only supposed to be a conception assignment, not a full-blown romance.

Marcel gave her a rakish grin. 'But you were the one who was keen to walk away and restart your normal life as soon as possible after the event, weren't you?'

She coloured. 'Well, in case I feel tired or... Marcel, you're supposed to be helping me stick to my resolve, not...'

'Darling, I'm sorry.' He sprang to his feet and leaned over her chair, his hands on the arms so that she couldn't escape. 'I was only teasing you. I'd planned all along to keep you with me all night. We don't want to rush things.'

He bent his head and kissed her gently on the lips before pulling himself to his full height.

He'd never called her 'darling' before. They were speaking English and his sexily husky French accent seemed to make the endearment sound particularly provocative. It crossed her mind that he must have called his wife 'darling' and she felt a pang of jealousy shooting through her.

She stood up. 'On the practical side. I'll check my menstrual calendar and work out when I'll be at my most fertile.'

'*Absolument!*' Marcel said with a whimsical smile on his face. 'After all, we don't want to waste time having to repeat our pregnancy assignments too many times before you become pregnant, do we?'

Debbie smiled as she sensed the implications of his remark. 'Marcel, you're wicked!'

'I know!' He drew her against him, holding her very close as he kissed her, this time more sensually.

She could feel her body reacting, feel the beating of

his heart against her white coat. She was wearing nothing but bra and pants underneath as it was a hot day, and she was feeling decidedly turned on by the closeness of his muscular body.

Marcel's pager vibrated against her from the breast pocket of his shirt. She jumped back.

Marcel groaned. 'This had better be important.' He hurried over to the door. 'Set up the time for the first assignment and I'll prepare the place.'

It was a whole week before her plans were finalised. She'd got the most fertile date written into her diary. She'd approached Francoise about staying the night, saying that she was going to spend the night with a friend who lived near the hospital.

Francoise, discreet as always, refrained from asking who the friend might be. If she had her suspicions, she didn't voice them. She was secretly hoping it might be that handsome doctor who'd called in and stitched up Emma's leg, but she would wait until she was told.

Debbie asked if Francoise would see Emma safely onto the school bus in the morning. Emma had started going on the bus at her own request as most of her friends did so. It made them feel more grown-up. Debbie explained that her mobile would be switched on.

Francoise agreed to everything.

When Debbie phoned Marcel to ask if the date was convenient, he said that he would move heaven and earth to fall in with her plans. She was the most important person in the equation because she would have to change her lifestyle during her pregnancy, whereas he would only have to be in at the conception.

Debbie said she had no intention of changing her lifestyle during her pregnancy. She would work until the very last minute. Pregnancy wasn't an illness. She was fit and healthy and it wouldn't make any difference. An argument ensued during which it almost seemed as if they might call the whole thing off.

At that point Marcel agreed that Debbie should decide what was best for her during her pregnancy. He ended the phone call amicably but determined to get his own way.

He was actually planning to become as involved with the pregnancy as Debbie would allow. He would have to ensure that she didn't become overtired. She had a tendency to keep going long after she should have downed tools and taken a rest.

And as for working until the last moment, the very idea appalled him! He was sure that he could persuade Debbie to see the reasoning behind his argument that she should take things easier when her pregnancy became more advanced.

On the evening of their so-called pregnancy assignment they both left the hospital together and drove up the hill in Marcel's car to his house. Marcel had told his *femme de ménage* that he was having a guest to stay the night and had asked that she prepare the guest room and also put clean sheets on his bed.

As Debbie walked into the house, she could feel butterflies churning around in the pit of her stomach. Marcel had suggested they have supper first. Debbie wasn't sure she could eat anything but decided to put on a show of normality. She sensed that they were both trying to pretend that it was perfectly normal to get together with the sole purpose of producing a child. And also…this was the most difficult bit!… to remain emotionally detached from the reproductive act. Impossible!

They had a light supper in the kitchen. Marcel

whisked up an omelette, Debbie tossed a salad. Marcel uncorked a bottle of claret.

'I laid this down for a special occasion,' he said as he poured some wine into her glass.

As Debbie raised the glass she could smell the delicious bouquet so typical of the Bordeaux region.

'Mmm, I love claret,' she said. 'The first red wine I was allowed as a young girl when I was taken by my father to a château near Bordeaux. My father allowed me a small taste from his glass. He told me it was a very good wine, so it always makes me nostalgic when I drink this type of wine.'

Marcel put down his fork. 'Nostalgic for the family life you enjoyed in spite of your parents not being together?'

She smiled. 'Yes, in some ways I had the best of both worlds, a doting father and an ever-present, dedicated mother.'

He leaned across the table and took hold of her hand. 'Our child will want for nothing. Our child will be loved by both of us.'

The touch of his hands sent a frisson of excitement running through her. Tonight…very soon now…she was going to lie in Marcel's arms. They were going to make love…all night if they wanted to…

Marcel caressed the palm of her hand. 'What are you smiling about?

'Was I smiling? I think it's because I'm happy. Because at last I may be able to begin the process of having another child,' she said quickly.

Marcel came around the table and drew her to her feet. 'Let's have our dessert later. I'll bring it up to bed…afterwards.'

He was holding her against him, his lips teasing hers.

She parted her lips and savoured his kiss, a kiss that was only the precursor of what was to come.

She sighed as he lifted her in his arms.

'Marcel, this is too romantic,' she whispered against his neck. 'Weren't we supposed to be trying to be unemotional?'

'Not good for the baby we're going to make. It's got to be conceived in love.' Marcel said huskily as he carried her out into the hall. 'For tonight we must pretend we're young lovers making love, without any thought of the future. And if we happen to have a baby…well, that will be a bonus, my darling.'

She relaxed against him as he carried her up the staircase into his bedroom. She'd dreamed of this moment. Already she'd abandoned all idea of putting any kind of restraint on her love-making. She was going to savour every magical moment…

At first when she opened her eyes she couldn't remember where she was. There was moonlight shining through the open casement window and the faint scent of roses from a garden. And then the wonderful memories came flooding back. She turned her head on the pillow and saw Marcel's dark hair close to hers.

He was still asleep, his breathing steady, a half-smile on his face. He looked as relaxed and happy as she herself felt. Mmm… She stretched out her legs beneath the sheet and twiddled her toes. She was still tingling from the ecstatic vibes of their love-making.

Marcel must have covered her with the sheet afterwards because she remembered quite clearly the sheet and quilt being tossed to the floor. What a wonderful lover he was! She'd never known such ecstasy. She remembered how he'd teased her, caressed her, explored every part of her body in the most tantalising way until she'd longed for him to take her completely so that she could experience the final fulfilment of their love-making.

When he'd first entered her, she'd cried out at the sheer joy of coupling with him, feeling him move inside her, throbbingly vibrant. And when she'd climaxed she'd cried out at the absolute heavenly ecstasy that had flooded through her entire body.

Marcel was stirring beside her now. She turned to look at him again and he opened his eyes. His mouth, his luscious sexy lips, those lips that had driven her to distraction during the night, now curved into a slow sensual smile.

He drew himself up onto one elbow, hovering above her, his eyes full of a deep tenderness she'd never seen before.

'You were sensational,' he whispered in English. 'Even if we don't have a baby, it was fun trying. No, it was more than fun. It was…'

He bent his head and kissed her, his lips as light as a feather. She felt her body stirring in response again. His kiss deepened. She sighed. Once more she was completely fluid, liquid, boneless, moving as one with her wonderful sexy lover, timeless, out of this world…no tomorrow…only today…

The early morning sun had drifted over the window-sill by the time Debbie woke again. Marcel stirred beside her and put out his hand to cradle hers.

She glanced at the clock. 'Time to get up, I think.' She was trying very hard to come down to earth. She was already longing for Marcel to take her in his arms again, but the longer she lingered here the more difficult it would be to pick up the threads of her everyday life.

'Don't go! I'll bring some coffee. We can spare ourselves a few more minutes of pretence.'

She hadn't the strength to argue. Debbie lay still, watching Marcel getting out of bed, shrugging himself into a white towelling dressing-gown. His muscular body was honed to perfection. She knew he worked out at the gym but she hadn't realised just how perfectly formed his fantastic, virile body was. She suppressed a sigh. The pretence that they were young lovers simply enjoying making love with each other was over. They had to get back to the real world and forget that they'd spent the night together.

She climbed out of bed and made for the bathroom. Stepping into the shower, she turned it on full so that the warm water cascaded over her. She had to get back to some sense of normality.

As she stepped out of the shower and reached for a white fluffy towel, she knew it wasn't going to be easy to put the events of the night from her mind. This was the point at which she had to walk away and go back to her everyday life as if nothing had happened. But something *had* happened. She was deeply, irrevocably in love, and there wasn't a thing she could do about it.

As for whether she was pregnant or not, she now had mixed feelings about that. That had been the object of them getting together initially. The reason for two very independent, uncommitted people to make a pact. One half of her was hoping that she was already pregnant, the other half hoped that they would need a further excuse to spend the night together.

'Coffee's ready!' Marcel called from the bedroom.

A second white towelling dressing-gown had been

placed on a stool near the shower. Debbie put it on. It was a woman's dressing-gown, a perfect fit for her. She felt another pang of jealousy. How many more females would wear this gown after her? She had no hold on Marcel. Only her child would have the privilege of being important to him.

Marcel was pouring the coffee as she walked back into the bedroom. He looked up and smiled.

'I'm glad you found the dressing-gown. You look stunning this morning.'

He was sitting in an armchair pulled close to a small table by the window. He stood up and pulled another chair close beside him.

'Come and join me.' He held out his arms and drew her against him. She tried to remain calm and composed but she could feel her body beneath the robe reacting to the nearness of this wonderful man.

'You're trembling,' he whispered, holding his lips against her cheek.

'It's the early morning chill.'

He pulled away and made to close the windows.

'No, don't do that. I love the scent of the roses from the garden. June is always a great month for roses. I remember as a child how my father always had roses in his garden during the summer...'

She chattered on about her childhood as Marcel poured the coffee. She was feeling totally confused now by her churning emotions, and she always chattered when she was nervous. She became silent again, losing herself in her disturbing thoughts about the future.

It was such an unnatural situation and for the moment she couldn't think how she was going to handle it. She'd thought she would be able to regain her senses easily, but she'd been mistaken. She realised that what she really wanted now was to cancel the whole idea that having a baby together was part of a contract, with set rules about caring for the child but no provision made for a loving relationship between the parents.

She wanted to change the contract. To rewrite the whole idea they'd dreamed up together and make everything much simpler…if marriage and family could ever be called simple! Looking across the small table at Marcel, she thought that it would never be simple but it would be the most wonderful life she could imagine.

How she'd changed! It was Marcel who had changed her. She couldn't imagine he would ever do anything deceitful. But wasn't that what she'd imagined about Paul until she realised she'd been taken in? Maybe the idea of being uncommitted really was the safest way of living. Definitely the safest, but was safety worth missing out on so much love?

Marcel placed a large breakfast cup of coffee in front of her. 'Would you like a croissant? They're fresh from the *boulangerie* delivery van. They always stop at the house in the mornings to see if I want a baguette or some croissants.'

'I'd love a croissant.' She broke into the crispy outer layer and added a teaspoonful of apricot jam.

'This is so civilised, having breakfast with you, Debbie.'

'Civilised?'

'Yes, we'll always be civilised when we meet in the future after our baby is born. That's what we planned, wasn't it?'

Debbie swallowed a morsel of the delicious croissant. 'Yes, we've got to look ahead at how we'll handle our lives,' she said carefully.

Marcel topped up her coffee-cup. 'Oh, it won't be a

problem. We're already getting back into our everyday selves, aren't we? You on one side of the table, me on the other, having our breakfast, discussing the roses and…'

He broke off and stretched his hand across the table to take hold of hers. He knew he was deluding himself. He didn't know how it was for Debbie, but he was finding it increasingly difficult! After their wonderful night of ecstasy when they'd lived the dream of being young lovers to perfection. But they'd agreed that neither of them wanted to commit to a real relationship, and for Debbie's sake he was going to honour their original plan.

Now, while they were both tingling with the aftermath of their love-making, wasn't the time to say that his ideas on the subject of their relationship were changing radically.

He stood up. 'I'll bring the car round to the front of the house. When you're ready we—'

'I'll be ready in ten minutes,' she said briskly, as she began loading the crockery onto a tray.

Their game of make-believe was over…until the next time. If they needed to meet for a next time, she thought as she stacked the cups. She couldn't help hoping this wasn't the last time she would spend the night with Marcel.

CHAPTER SIX

As the days passed by and the date when her period was due drew nearer, Debbie found she was on tenterhooks. She had mixed feelings about the possibility that she might be pregnant. The ultimate dream of having a second child had to be weighed against the fact that she would no longer have an excuse to spend another wonderful night with Marcel.

For the first few days after their night together, Marcel had seemed to be making it quite clear that he was sticking to their plan. At the hospital he was ultra-professional with her. Occasionally he would slip down to her office for a coffee and a chat, mostly about work, but he hadn't suggested they meet outside the hospital so she'd come to terms with the fact that this was what her future held. A platonic friendship with her baby's father.

The joy of having another baby would be infinite. If only she hadn't agreed not to fall in love with the baby's father!

And then one morning when she arrived in Urgences there was a message in Reception to say that Marcel wanted to see her in his office as soon as she arrived.

'What's the problem?' she asked as she sat down in the chair beside his desk.

He switched off his computer. 'The weather,' he said, standing up and coming round to her side of the desk. 'We're well into the summer and we haven't made the most of it. Look at that glorious sunshine!'

He waved his arm towards the window.

'Yes, it's lovely out there but we're on duty so—'

'No, we're not. Everything's quiet this morning so I've cleared our work schedules. You and I are off duty unless we get an urgent call that the rest of the medical staff can't handle.'

Debbie's eyes widened. 'What brought this on?'

'I'm giving my staff in Urgences an extra day off duty when the weather is good. I suggested to the board of directors that it would be good for morale. Everybody is getting fed up with being inside when the weather is so glorious. The chairman thought it would be an excellent idea and asked me to arrange it. We'll all take our off-duty days at different times, of course, but providing the department is well staffed and that we agree to return should an emergency arise, there will be no problem.'

'Sounds good to me. So the two of us are to start the scheme today, are we?'

She was trying to sound calm about it, but the fact that Marcel had included her in his day off duty was encouraging. Did it mean the two of them might have a life beside the baby plan?

'I'm going to take you on a tour of the coast till we reach a good beach for swimming. Then we'll have lunch in a small restaurant I know, returning here later this afternoon to check that everything's running smoothly.'

'I wish you'd phoned me about this. I haven't got anything to wear for swimming.'

'I only got the OK from the board of directors a few minutes ago so you would have left home by then. No problem. We'll drive into Le Touquet on our way and pick up a swimsuit at one of the shops. I've got some beach towels in my cupboard here at the hospital so we're all set.'

'You've thought of everything.' She smiled. 'I like the idea of buying a new swimsuit. I've been meaning to buy a new bikini all through the summer but I never got around to it. Last weekend on the beach with Emma I realised the fabric of the one I was wearing was completely washed out with the effect of the sea water.'

'Can Emma swim?'

'Oh, yes!' Debbie said proudly. 'She's getting really good at it.'

'Pity she's at school or we could have taken her with us. I'd like to get to know your daughter. After all, I'll probably see her quite often if we succeed in having a baby.'

Debbie had a moment of anxiety. 'We'll have to be careful about that. Emma said she didn't want another daddy. Even though she never sees her own father, she believes that he loves her and that nobody could take his place. Your visits will probably also make her wonder even more about why her own father doesn't come and visit.'

Marcel placed a finger under Debbie's chin, raising her face so that she had to look him in the eye.

'We'll be extremely careful and, believe me, Debbie, I would never try to take Emma's father's place. She has treasured ideas about her father and I hope nothing will ever shatter them. I'll be her friend if she wants me to be.' He hesitated. 'I feel so impatient to know if we've already been successful.'

Debbie smiled up at him. 'So do I. My period's due at the weekend. I'll let you know if it arrives.'

'If it doesn't, we'll have to try again,' he said huskily.

She felt a stirring of desire as he moved closer.

'It was a wonderful night we spent together, Debbie.'

It was the first time he'd alluded to what had passed between them. Since arriving back at the hospital on the morning after their night together, she'd almost imagined she'd dreamed the whole experience. But, yes, it had truly happened and it had been wonderful. Too wonderful! She hadn't meant to be so moved. She'd thought she could handle her emotions better than she was doing.

'So, let's get going,' she said, quickly, anxious not to give way to her feelings.

Marcel drove into Le Touquet and parked in a large car park beside the beach. They had a coffee in a small bar sitting on the terrace overlooking the sea. The sun was streaming down on them and Marcel adjusted the parasol that shaded their table. Although it was only the middle of the morning Debbie was surprised to see that the beach was crowded with holidaymakers.

'It's the height of the season,' Marcel said. 'We'll find a quieter beach for our swim.'

She put down her coffee-cup and began to unwrap one of the tiny ginger biscuits that had arrived with the coffee. 'After I've bought my bikini.'

'You must let me buy it for you. It's an early birthday present. Your birthday's in September, isn't it?'

She looked surprised. 'You've been checking up on me.'

'It was on the curriculum vitae you sent in when you started work at the hospital. It's your thirtieth birthday, isn't it?'

'Don't remind me!'

'You're still very young. I'm thirty-eight already.'

'Yes, but you're a man!'

'Ah, so you noticed!'

She laughed. 'What I meant was that men can father children until they're well into old age.'

Marcel grinned. 'Yes, but as you know I'm impatient. That's why I've already made a start with someone who looks as if she'll make the perfect mother.'

He stood up and drew her to her feet. 'Come on, let's go and get your bikini.'

They walked down one of the side streets that led to the beach, Debbie stopping to look into each of the shop windows as they passed. And then she saw it.

'That's the one!'

The white bikini was on a model in the centre of the window. It was two tiny scraps of material with gold rings at each side of the hips and through the centre of the bra.

'So long as you don't adopt that awful smug expression the model is wearing you'll look great in it.'

Debbie laughed. 'I promise I won't.'

Marcel followed her into the little boutique and sat on a chair in the corner feeling decidedly out of place in this very feminine shop. He stared studiously out of the window as Debbie told the saleswoman she'd like to try on the white bikini in the window. After she'd disappeared into a cubicle, Marcel thumbed his way through one of the magazines on the small wrought-iron table.

He was surprised to find a news magazine among the beauty and fashion magazines spread out for the female clientele. Probably meant for male escorts like himself. He hoped Debbie wouldn't take too long. He wanted to get out into the fresh air again. The cloying air freshener was tickling his nostrils.

Debbie emerged smiling, carrying the bikini. Marcel felt relieved that she'd made her mind up so quickly.

His credit card was already in his hand and he moved to the cash desk.

'*Merci, monsieur*,' the saleswoman said, handing over a receipt.

'It's perfect!' Debbie said as she watched the sales-woman placing it in a packet with the name of the bou-tique emblazoned on the outside.

'Thank you so much, Marcel,' she said, as they went outside. 'It's so lovely. I can't wait to put it on.'

'I can't wait to see you in it.'

He took hold of her hand and they walked back to the car.

Driving up the coast, Debbie lay back against her seat. Marcel had let down the hood of his silver sports car and the breeze was tumbling her long dark hair be-hind her as he increased his speed.

He took one hand off the wheel and reached for hers. 'I'm glad we took the day off, aren't you?'

'Mmm! This is the life! At times like this I can't think why I ever wanted to be a career-woman.'

'You could always give it all up and become a full-time mother.'

'Only if I had the money.'

'If that was what you wanted, I'm sure we could find a solution.'

'Don't even think about it,' she said, firmly, wishing she hadn't made her flippant remark about giving up her career. 'I'll never be a kept woman. I'll always work outside the home. I need to be fully independent for the rest of my life.'

'I know…and I admire you for it, but…'

He dropped the car down a gear as he drove round a narrow bend. He'd said too much already. Debbie was Debbie and would never change. He'd known that when they'd first agreed on their idea for a baby. He'd been lucky she'd agreed to the plan. But their plan of no commitment had to stand firm.

He turned off the main road and drove down a small lane that led to a quiet sandy cove. The beach was almost deserted. They found a quiet spot at the edge of the sand-hills and Marcel spread towels on the sand.

Debbie wrapped a towel round her as she changed into the white bikini.

'You look fantastic! It suits you much better than that miserable model in the window.'

Debbie smiled. 'Come on, I'll race you to the sea.'

They ran down. Marcel deliberately stayed beside her until the last few steps when he increased his pace and surged ahead. Watching his lithe, muscular body in the black swimming shorts streaking ahead of her made her feel excited. Excited in the knowledge that she was going to know this man all her life. He was going to be part of her child's life and she would always be able to contact him.

It wasn't ideal but it was all that was possible under the circumstances.

They swam out to a rock some way from the shore. Clambering up the warm surface, Debbie found she was breathless with the exertion. She clung to the stone surface as she lay down on her stomach, gazing down into the swirling waves. The sun was warm on her back.

'The sea's still quite cool,' she said, as Marcel lay down beside her, raising himself on one elbow so he could look down at her.

'It's a good thing the sun is warm.' Debbie said. 'My skin is cold.'

He bent down and covered her body with his. 'Are you feeling warmer now?'

She looked up into his eyes, so full of tenderness. 'I'm much warmer.'

She could feel herself relaxing against him. He was taking all his weight on his elbows but his skin, lightly touching hers was evocative of what had already passed between them.

He lowered his head and kissed her gently on the lips. She responded, parting her lips so that she could savour the moment.

Marcel pulled himself away. 'It's hardly an ideal spot for romance, perched on this precarious rock.'

She sat up, hugging her knees. 'Are we going to allow ourselves romance when we meet in the future?'

'I sincerely hope so! I would find it very hard to meet up with you and not feel romantic!'

'So we're going to have a platonic yet romantic relationship for the sake of our child—is that it?'

He smiled. 'Do you think that would work?'

'Sounds like you're hoping for the best of both worlds. Independence and occasional romantic liaisons.'

He shifted his position on the rock so that he was in a sitting position. 'That about sums it up. Would you agree to that?'

She smiled. 'Sounds like we're having a board meeting.'

Marcel laughed. 'Great place for a meeting, sitting on a rock surrounded by the sea with the summer sun warm on our bodies.'

He leaned forward and caressed her cheek. 'Years from now we'll remember this meeting when our child is growing up. The day we agreed on independence and occasional romance. You do think that would work, don't you, Debbie?'

She nodded. It was good to know that Marcel was

looking so far ahead. But their future plans were so nebulous. Would occasional romance satisfy her? In her heart of hearts she knew it wouldn't be enough, but she would have to go along with it.

Marcel stood up and drew her to her feet. 'Let's go back to shore. Careful on the edge of the rock here. It's very slippery. Keep hold of my hand and I'll help you down…'

They swam back to shore side by side, running up the beach to dry themselves and get dressed.

'Where are we going for lunch?' Debbie asked as she ran a comb through her tousled hair.

'I know a little restaurant on the edge of the sand-hills over on that side of the beach. Should take us about ten minutes to walk there. Very small, family-run place,' he said as they set off along the beach, 'and the food is excellent.'

The proprietor, Henri, and his wife, Antoinette, greeted Marcel like a long-lost friend.

'Oh, Dr De Lange, *quel plaisir*!' Antoinette said, bustling out of the kitchen, wiping her hands down her apron. 'Henri told me you were here. As soon as you telephoned this morning I reserved your favourite table for you.'

The plump dimpled cheeks were smiling as Antoinette shook hands with Marcel, turning to acknowledge Debbie with a polite '*Bonjour, madame.*'

They were quickly seated at a table by the window. In the centre of the red and white gingham cloth was a small glass vase containing a single red rose.

The proprietor leaned forward, pointing to the rose, and whispered something in Marcel's ear.

Marcel smiled. '*C'est parfait,* Henri!'

Their aperitifs were on the house. Debbie chose kir,

her favourite, made from white wine and *crème de cassis*. Marcel asked for a glass of Pernod. As he poured in the water he swirled his glass so that it turned cloudy. Raising his glass towards Debbie, he said, in English, 'Here's to the success of our plan.'

Debbie smiled. 'I'll drink to that.'

She felt a sudden qualm of anxiety. She glanced around the room. Two other couples were nearby but they were intent on their own conversations. She lowered her voice.

'I hope I'm going to be able to deliver the goods, so to speak. What will happen if we find problems in—?'

'Let's think positive!' He reached across the table and took hold of her hand. 'If there's a medical hitch, we'll face it together. We're both in good health. Let's just enjoy trying. That wasn't a problem, was it?'

She could feel herself blushing. Henri had arrived with their starters and was placing some *pâté de fois gras* in front of her. She took a piece of thin toast from the warmed napkin and spread some of the pâté on it.

'Delicious!' she said, looking across at Marcel. 'How's your *saumon fumé*?'

Marcel pronounced his smoked salmon superb.

'I love the rose in the centre of the table,' Debbie said. 'Was that your idea?'

He smiled. 'What makes you think that?'

'You're a romantic.'

'I'll take that as a compliment.'

'It was meant to be.'

As they looked at each other across the table Debbie felt her heart beating faster. She could imagine meeting up with Marcel in the future, enjoying lunch or dinner in a restaurant. Going to the theatre or a concert. During the course of their conversations during the past weeks,

they'd both discovered their mutual interest in the theatre and music. It could work out between them. Independence and romance.

She tried to convince herself that it was the only kind
of relationship for two independent people still suffering
from the scars of their previous relationships.

'You're looking very solemn all of a sudden,' Marcel
said.

'Am I? I was thinking about the future, our future.
What it will be like when we meet from time to time.'

Henri arrived with their main courses, and for a few
moments their conversation came to a standstill.

'I should imagine it will be something like this,'
Marcel said, picking up his steak knife. 'Except we'll
have our child with us.'

'In a high chair, throwing food on the floor,' Debbie
said lightly.

Marcel laughed. 'I can't wait to be a proper father.
That will be fun.'

Debbie was glad she'd eased the tension by making
an attempt at a joke. She reasoned she ought to stop
worrying about the future otherwise she would put a
damper on their day out together. It was no good constantly looking ahead to the problems they might en-
counter. Much better to live for the moment where her
relationship with Marcel was concerned. Simply take
each day as it came. Because each precious moment
with Marcel was worth savouring.

She enjoyed her pheasant cooked in Calvados, which
was a regional dish from Normandy. Marcel declared
that his steak was perfectly grilled, just as he liked it.

Debbie had decided to skip dessert, feeling replete,
but Antoinette hurried out of the kitchen carrying her
home-made *tarte maison* which she'd just taken from

the oven. The smell of the home-grown apples and shortcrust pastry was too tempting so Debbie changed her mind. After dessert they were served with coffee on the terrace facing the sea.

Marcel took hold of her hand. 'I think we've resolved a great deal today.'

Debbie looked up at him. 'Have we?'

'Yes, I feel more…er…comfortable with our relationship now.'

'Comfortable?'

'I think we've ironed out the creases. We know where we're going.'

She leaned forward. 'All I've got to do now is get pregnant.'

He drew closer and kissed the side of her cheek. 'Let's hope that's already been accomplished.'

'I'll let you know as soon as I'm sure.'

Marcel drove back slowly to the hospital. It was as if they were both winding down from what had been a memorable day together. Debbie knew she didn't want to get back. She wanted to prolong her time alone with Marcel. She began thinking about all the occasions in the future when their times alone would be so limited. Quickly she checked her thoughts again. No more looking into the future. Live for today and enjoy it while you could.

Everything was running smoothly when they got back at the hospital late in the afternoon. There had, however, been one car crash where two patients had been brought in, but they were both in Theatre. The only patients now in Urgences were being treated and the medical staff had everything under control.

Debbie went into the treatment room to help the plaster nurse fix a cast on a fractured ulna. The young woman patient had fallen from her bicycle, putting out her right hand to prevent her fall and cracking the bigger of the two bones in the forearm.

'I feel such an idiot,' the patient said, as she looked up at Debbie. 'One minute I'm cycling along and the next, just because a dog ran in front of my wheel, I'm stretched out on the road. Why on earth did I put my hand out like that? I should have simply rolled and then I would have been OK.'

'If it's any consolation, Susanne,' Debbie told the patient, 'this often happens to people who fall. It's a natural instinct to put out your hand as you go down.'

She pointed to the X-rays highlighted on the wall. 'Your injury is typical of the ones I've seen since I first began my training in orthopaedics. And the good news is that the majority of these injuries heal very quickly. In four or five weeks you'll have your cast off and your arm will be as good as new.'

'Thanks, Doctor. Will you be taking my cast off?'

'I'm referring you to our orthopaedic department now. You'll have an appointment to see the consultant and he'll take over your treatment.'

Debbie's next patient was a twelve-year-old boy who'd landed heavily on the side of a trampoline as he'd been bouncing up and down in the garden. His back was badly bruised. Debbie checked out his nerve responses. There didn't seem to be any serious neural damage, but she made a call to the neurology department, explaining the case history and asking that the boy be admitted for further neurological tests. You couldn't be too careful with back injuries, which were on the increase now since trampolines had become so popular.

Next she treated a small child who'd pushed a bead into his ear. When she investigated with an auriscope, she could see the bead wedged up against the eardrum. Very carefully, with a pair of long tapering forceps, she was able to dislodge the bead and pull it out of the outer ear.

'Your little boy has been very lucky that the bead didn't perforate the eardrum,' she told the mother as she handed her the bead. 'Do you want to keep this as a souvenir?'

The mother smiled. 'I don't think so. Put it in the bin, Doctor. I'm going to get rid of that box of beads when I get home. It's been such a terrible time for us. Thank you so much. You were brilliant. I thought he'd have to stay in and have an operation.'

As Debbie said goodbye, she didn't tell the mother that she herself had been extremely relieved when she'd successfully manoeuvred the bead out of the narrow external auditory meatus. It had needed a very steady hand not to damage the eardrum.

'It's time you were off duty,' Marcel said, standing in the doorway of the treatment room.

She glanced at the clock. 'So it is.' She began clearing up the instruments she'd used.

'Leave that. I'll finish off in here. You need to get home to Emma.'

'Thanks.'

She made for the door. He put one hand on the wall above her as she came through, effectively blocking the doorway. They were standing in a busy area, with doctors and nurses moving in every direction. Marcel knew there was no chance of kissing Debbie goodbye, but he could delay her for a few moments.

He looked down at her. 'It's been a great day,' he said quietly. 'Thank you.'

She smiled. 'I enjoyed it.'

He took his hand from the wall so that she could go through. He watched as she walked quickly away without looking back. She looked strong, self-assured, independent, the sort of woman who would always know her own mind, never wavering in her decisions. Especially the important decision never to commit herself to another man again.

He took a deep breath. He was going to honour their original plan but, after spending the day with Debbie, he was finding his resolve was decidedly wavering. But as he went over to the treatment trolley to check on the instruments, he told himself that when he'd first married Lisa he'd thought that his feelings would never change. And how wrong he'd been! He was lucky that he'd found someone like Debbie who was of the same mind as he was.

Debbie woke early on Saturday morning. She could tell at once that her period had arrived. She was always as regular as clockwork so she was totally prepared. Only this time she'd hoped that it might not happen. So she wasn't pregnant after all. Well, that would mean another pregnancy assignment, to give it the technical name she and Marcel had invented. Another night of making love was how she hoped it would be.

As she hurried out to the bathroom she realised how much she was looking forward to it. Later that morning she would phone Marcel and give him the news that he wasn't going to be a father—yet.

After her shower she went along to Emma's room. Her little daughter smiled as she opened her eyes and wriggled into a sitting position, holding her arms wide for a cuddle. She might be six years old but she was still Debbie's baby. She still had that definitive baby scent about her, kiddy jimjams, baby talcum powder, sleep. It was difficult to quantify but it was the scent of her own child. And, hopefully, she might have another baby within the foreseeable future.

Debbie pulled away and smoothed down her daughter's tousled blonde hair. She was still as fair-haired as her father was. She preferred to think that Emma took after her mother. She had Paul's high cheekbones and slightly pointed chin, but that was where the resemblance ended. Her personality was completely different—thank goodness!

Debbie busied herself putting out Emma's clothes.

'Would you like to wear your new shorts?'

'Ooh, yes, please.' Emma jumped out of bed and hurried over to stand beside her chest of drawers. 'And this T-shirt, the one with the fishes on that we got in that shop by the sea. Can we go to the sea today, Mummy? I want to swim and swim and swim!'

Emma was hopping on one foot now, happily singing a song she was making up as she went along, something she loved to do when she was happy.

'And the fishes will come up and tickle my toes and I will swim and swim and...'

'Put your clothes on and come down for breakfast, darling. I need to work out what's happening today. I expect we can fit in a trip to the beach for a couple of hours.'

Hurrying down the stairs a little later, Debbie knew she would have to make that phone call to Marcel. She'd promised to give him the news as soon as she knew.

In the kitchen she put the kettle on before picking up the phone.

He took the news in an objective sort of way. 'Oh, well, we'll have to try again. I'm disappointed, of course, but… Just a moment while I look in my diary. I worked out your next fertile period in case we needed another assignment, so now I have to see… Have you got your diary with you, Debbie?'

Her diary was always next to the phone when she was at home. She picked it up. Over the phone she could hear the sound of pages being turned.

'Yes, that would be excellent,' Marcel said.

'What would?' she asked.

'I've been thinking it would be fun to go to Paris for our next assignment. I know a wonderfully romantic little hotel in the sixteenth arrondissement. Right down by the Seine. You can sit on the balcony and watch the boats going past. How would you feel about that, Debbie? Don't you think it would be fantastic if you conceived our baby in Paris?'

She felt bowled over with excitement, but decided she should dampen down her enthusiasm. 'I…er…I don't know what to say.'

'Just say yes! And then we can sort out the most convenient date for you.'

She smiled. After a depressing start to her day it was good to hear Marcel enthusing about a trip to Paris. She felt her spirits lifting. A night in Paris with Marcel. What could be more romantic?

'Debbie, are you still there? You're probably thinking it's a mad idea, but we would always remember if our child was conceived in Paris, wouldn't we?'

'Marcel, I'm hooked on the idea already.'

'Great! I'll make the reservation. Now, there's the

little question of the exact date. I'll arrange for us to take two days off midweek, so if you could check your diary for the week beginning...'

'Just a moment, Marcel, I can't hear you above Emma's singing...'

Emma had come dancing into the kitchen, still singing loudly about the sea and the fishes and the sun.

'Mummy, Mummy, can we leave now?'

'I'll call you back, Marcel, when—'

'Mummy, is that the nice doctor who stitched my leg? Can I say hello to him?'

'Emma would like to speak to you, Marcel.'

'And I'd like to speak to Emma.'

Debbie thought he sounded pleased. She handed over the phone.

Emma beamed. 'Hello, Marcel. It's me, Emma.'

Debbie hovered close by, shamelessly eavesdropping on their conversation. She could only guess what Marcel was saying.

Emma was listening to Marcel's voice before volunteering the information that they were going to the beach.

'Would you like to come with us, Marcel?' Emma added. 'You'll have to bring your swimming costume and— Oh, no...'

She turned to look at Debbie. 'Marcel says he's on duty at the hospital today, but he'd love to come next weekend if that's OK with you.'

Debbie smiled. 'That would be lovely.'

Emma told Marcel what Debbie had said before she continued to chatter. It sounded as if Marcel was asking about her leg.

'Oh, it's fine now. Mummy took the stitches out and it tickled. But I've got a scar. Mummy says it will disappear in time but I don't want it to. It looks very cool. Do you know the word ''cool''? I don't know how to say it in French… Oh, that's OK then.'

She turned to Debbie. 'Marcel says they now use the English word ''cool'' in France. Did you know that, Mummy?'

'Yes, I did. Emma, I think Marcel will be very busy as he's on duty.'

'Mummy says I've got to go now. OK, I'll get her. Bye.'

Emma handed over the phone.

'She's gorgeous, your daughter,' Marcel said. 'I'm glad you've given me permission to come with you to the beach next weekend. I'll look forward to it. And I'll look forward to our date in Paris. Give me a call this evening when you've sorted out your diary.'

She put down the phone and turned to hug her daughter. Emma would be so thrilled if she had a baby brother or sister. Since Emma had said she didn't want another daddy, she'd worried that Emma might consider Marcel, the baby's father, as having designs on becoming her father as well. She'd also worried about how Emma would feel about not having her own daddy around, too. But now that Emma and Marcel seemed to be bonding, with careful handling it might not be too much of a problem.

She reminded herself to stop looking too far ahead. She would take one step at a time. For the moment her priority was Emma, to make sure she had the happiest childhood possible.

'We'll go to the sea as soon as we've had breakfast, Emma. Would you carry this jar of jam to the table for me? That's a good girl. Careful, careful…'

CHAPTER SEVEN

THE following weekend, Debbie packed a picnic lunch in preparation for their day on the beach. Emma was tremendously excited about the fact that Marcel was going to pick them up in his sports car. When she heard the sound of a car pulling into the drive she was beside herself with excitement, jumping down from her place at the kitchen table and running out of the door to meet him.

Her eyes widened as she admired the silver sports car with the top down. 'Wow, are we really going to drive to the beach in that? Can I sit in the front?'

Marcel was smiling happily as he climbed out of the driver's seat. 'I don't think that would be a good idea, Emma. The seat at the back is better for you. It's too small for a grown-up so Mummy had better sit in the front with me. Hello, Debbie.'

'Hi, there!' Debbie hovered in the doorway. 'Did you have breakfast, Marcel? We had a late start and we're still finishing off.'

'I had some coffee.'

'Come and have some more. And maybe a croissant? I bought too many at the *boulangerie* this morning.'

Marcel followed Debbie into the kitchen.

'Come and sit next to me here, Marcel,' Emma said, grabbing his hand and directing him to his allotted place at the table.

It felt so right to be sitting round the kitchen table with her daughter chattering away to Marcel. He was working his way through a croissant, sipping his coffee and all the time listening intently to the story that Emma was telling him about her school.

'When I go back to school in September, I won't be in the baby class. I'll be in the bigger children's class and all the new children will be in the classroom I've just left. My teacher in my new classroom is very pretty. She's very young, much younger than Mummy, I think.'

'Your mummy's still young,' Marcel said solemnly, licking some apricot jam from his bottom lip.

Emma giggled as she took a sip of her orange juice. 'Mummy looks young but she's old really. She's nearly thirty. My new teacher's only about…er…sixteen, I think.'

Debbie smiled. 'She's twenty-two, actually. And, yes, she's very pretty.'

'Would I think she was pretty?' Marcel asked lightly.

'Oh, you'd think she was gorgeous!' Emma said. 'Because you're a man. Have you got a wife?'

'No.'

'Girlfriend?'

Marcel glanced across the kitchen to where Debbie was stacking the dishwasher. She turned to look at him.

'There's a woman I'm very fond of,' he said, slowly. 'But grown-up relationships are never as easy as you imagine when you're a child.'

'Well, have you got any children?' Emma wasn't going to let him get off the hook easily.

'Not yet,' he said quietly.

Emma pulled a wry face. 'It's a pity you haven't got any children. You could have brought them with you to play with me. I asked Mummy ages ago if I could have a baby sister like my friend Céline's got, but Mummy said she hasn't got a daddy to make a baby with. The daddy has to plant the seed in the mummy, you see. Did you know that, Marcel?'

Marcel nodded solemnly. 'Yes, I'm a doctor so I have to know about these things.'

Emma looked thoughtful. 'I suppose you do. Because you have to get the babies out of the mummies' tummies, don't you?'

'Yes, I do.' Marcel took a long drink from his coffee-cup while he prepared himself for the next question.

Emma fixed him with an intense look. 'Do you ever have any babies lying around that nobody wants to take home with them? I mean, if you did, could you bring one here? I'd look after it ever so well, take it out for walks and when it's bigger it could play with me, couldn't it?'

'I'm sorry, Emma, but I never have any babies to spare,' Marcel said solemnly.

Debbie closed the door of the dishwasher. 'I'm afraid you'll just have to make do with Marcel and me as playmates on the beach today, Emma. Have you packed your swimsuit in your rucksack? Let's go and check, shall we?'

She wasn't sure where Emma's questions would lead next, and she didn't feel she could handle any more explanations in front of Marcel.

As they walked out of the front door, he reached for her hand and squeezed it. Emma ran ahead excitedly and climbed into the back seat.

Debbie looked up at Marcel and whispered, 'I didn't think it was a good time to start explanations about the fact that I've found a man to father my child. It's not going to be easy to explain our complicated situation.'

He put an arm round her waist. 'If and when we find

a baby is on the way, will you let me help you with the answers to Emma's questions?'

'Absolutely! I'll need all the help I can get. At least I don't have to worry about whether she likes you or not. She seems besotted.'

Marcel smiled. 'The feeling's mutual. I wish she was my daughter.'

Debbie swallowed hard. So did she. She still couldn't be sure how Emma would react if Marcel became father to her second child.

As she climbed into the passenger seat she found herself fantasising about how wonderful it would be if they were a real family setting out for a day at the beach. The baby strapped into its special seat, their elder child sitting beside her baby sister—or would it be a brother? It didn't matter so long as it was their longed-for, much-cherished baby. And Marcel, the doting father, starting up the engine as he was doing now...

'Are you OK, Debbie?' Marcel asked, touching the back of her hand as he drove out. 'You look as if you're far away somewhere.'

'No, I'm right here with you. Just thinking, that's all.'

They found a quiet spot on the edge of the sand-hills at a nearby beach. There were a few families on the beach but it wasn't crowded. Emma spread the travel rug on the sand and began opening up the picnic basket.

'Not yet, darling,' Debbie said. 'We've only just had breakfast. The food will stay fresher if we leave it in the cool bag. Come and show Marcel what a good swimmer you are.'

Once Emma was in the water it was difficult to tempt her back on dry land again. She was an excellent little swimmer but she had to be supervised the whole time to ensure she didn't stray out of her depth.

Marcel stayed with her for the rest of the morning, teaching her how to improve her arm and leg movements and then simply having fun splashing around. Emma insisted on climbing on his back, pretending he was a big fish and she was a mermaid who wanted a lift. Debbie, who was now sitting on the sand with a towel wrapped round her shoulders, smiled as she watched the two of them playing together.

Marcel was so patient with Emma! And he had such energy! She wouldn't have the strength to keep going as long as he did in this game of make-believe. It looked as if Marcel had now been turned into a shark that was required to snap its jaws at Emma. She was screaming with delight as he began to chase her out of the shallow water towards the beach.

'Come on, Emma, I'll race you back to the shark's camp,' he said, winking at Debbie as the two of them streaked past her.

'Sharks don't have camps,' Emma said, puffing loudly as she tried to keep up with Marcel.

'This shark has a camp up near the sand-hills,' Marcel said, slowing his pace so that Emma would have no difficulty in running beside him. 'He's got lots of food that little girls like.'

Marcel turned his head as he heard Debbie running after them. 'What do little girls like to eat, Debbie?'

'Some of them like ice cream from my special container,' Debbie said.

'Yes, I love ice cream!' Emma said, shedding her mermaid role. 'Do you like ice cream, Marcel?'

'One of my favourite foods!'

Emma, with renewed energy, was now streaking ahead, shouting, 'I'm the winner! I'm the winner!'

Marcel turned to look at Debbie. 'I've got some ham baguettes in the cool box of my holdall. And a bottle of wine, some peaches, but no ice cream.'

'I've brought a cooked chicken and some salad so we've got everything we could possibly need.'

Marcel reached for her hand. 'We have indeed. I couldn't wish for anything more.' He lowered his voice. 'That must be the sexiest bikini I have ever seen. But it's what's in it that makes it look so stunning.'

'Thank you. It's a fabulous birthday present.'

'I'll buy you something else on your actual birthday in September. Maybe…I don't know, something significant. Perhaps there might be something significant to celebrate by then.'

'I hope there is,' she said, as they reached their camp near the sand-hills. Emma had already dried herself and put on a dry swimsuit just as Debbie had shown her so many times when she came out of the sea. Her little swimsuit was hung precariously over the branch of a gorse bush.

'What a good girl you are,' Debbie said, hugging her daughter. 'I do love you.'

Emma smiled happily. 'I love you, Mummy.'

Watching mother and daughter hugging each other, Marcel wanted to join them and tell them that he loved them both. But he held back. How often would he have to hold back in the future? This wasn't his family, however much he wished it was. He was hoping he would father Debbie's baby but he would have to be careful not to overstep the mark. It was going to be so difficult to define his role in this family.

He reached down into the holdall he'd carried from

the car. 'Ham roll, anyone?' he said, dispensing the baguettes from his cool bag.

Debbie cut pieces from the chicken and placed them on plastic plates. Marcel uncorked the wine and handed her a glass as she picked up the salad servers to toss the salad in the plastic bowl.

'Let me toss the salad, Mummy.' Emma took the salad servers from her mother, sloshing the prepared vinaigrette into the bowl.

'Not too much vinaigrette, Emma,' Debbie said, as she took a sip of her wine. 'Mmm, I love the wine.'

'It's another Bordeaux vintage. I remembered you enjoyed the one we drank at Henri and Antoinette's restaurant.'

He touched his plastic glass against hers. 'Tastes better when drunk from a real glass, but we're on a picnic and I didn't think the glasses would survive being bashed around on the beach.'

'Emma, I think you've tossed the salad enough now, darling. It's ready to be served.'

Emma grinned as she put down the wooden salad servers. 'What did my Grandpapa André say when he taught me to toss the salad, Mummy?'

Debbie smiled. 'Grandpapa André said that "*quand on est assez grand pour tourner la salade on est assez grand pour se marier.*"'

Emma looked up at Marcel. 'You know what that means, don't you, because you're French?'

Marcel smiled. 'It means when you're big enough to toss the salad you're big enough to get married.'

Emma giggled. 'I'm not going to get married. I'm going to be a doctor like mummy, and doctors don't have time to get married, do they?'

'Some of them do,' Marcel said quietly.

'Yes, but Mummy told me she's happy on her own, just looking after me, didn't you, Mummy?'

'Yes, I did, Emma. Would you like some ice cream now?'

'Oh, yes, please.'

After lunch Debbie and Marcel stretched out on the sand, enjoying the sun. Debbie rubbed a high-factor sun cream into Emma's skin as she curled up between them. Debbie closed her eyes. It was so peaceful, she found herself dropping off to sleep…

She became aware that Marcel was standing in front of her as she opened her eyes.

He leaned down, speaking softly so as not to wake Emma up. 'I've had a call from the hospital so I'd better get back. I promised to do some extra time if I was needed this weekend. I'm making up the time I'll be taking during our two days in Paris.'

'Do you want me to make up any time during this week?'

'No, I've taken your two days from your legitimate off-duty days. But as the boss I've got to put in a bit extra. Sorry to break up the beach party but I'd better run you home now.'

He put out a hand and drew her to her feet. Gently he slid his arms around her waist and held her close, touching her lips lightly with his own.

'I've enjoyed being part of your family for a few hours,' he said quietly as he pulled himself away.

Debbie held her breath. She wanted to say how she wished he really was part of her family, but she didn't dare.

'You've been wonderful with Emma. Worn her out!'

As if hearing her name, Emma opened her eyes.

'Emma, darling, we've got to go home now. Will you collect your swimsuit from over there and—?'

'Is Marcel coming with us?'

'I've got to go back to the hospital, but I'll drive you home first.'

'Can't you stay for supper?'

'Sorry, Emma, some other time perhaps.'

It was the end of a perfect day, Debbie thought as she tucked Emma into bed. In spite of the nap on the beach, her daughter was tired enough to go to bed early and fall asleep immediately. Debbie went downstairs and began clearing up the picnic things she'd dumped in the kitchen. The phone rang.

'Thanks, Debbie. It was a great picnic.'

Her spirits soared at the sound of Marcel's voice. 'We enjoyed it. Emma's asleep already. Where are you?'

'I'm at the hospital, having a break between patients. I found myself thinking about our trip to Paris. It's all fixed. They've promised to put us in a room overlooking the river.'

'Sounds wonderful!'

'It will be…' He broke off and she heard him talking to someone. She also heard the noise of a trolley being wheeled nearby, somebody coughing violently. 'I've got to go. See you on Monday.'

Debbie heard the click of his phone at the other end. Her spirits drooped again. Usually she enjoyed a quiet Saturday night after Emma had gone to sleep. Sometimes she watched a video she wanted to see, often she simply curled up with a good book and some background music on the radio.

But tonight she didn't want to be alone. She would have liked to phone Marcel and say that whatever time he finished she hoped he would come over and join her. Even better, he could stay all night, share breakfast with her in the morning.

She felt a tear pricking behind her eyelids. This independent yet romantic relationship wasn't going to work in its present form. But what was the alternative? Frighten Marcel away by saying that she wanted him to make a commitment to stay with her for the rest of their lives?

She couldn't do that to him. Couldn't risk shattering the delicate balance of the friendship they had. She had to go along with their agreement.

The day of their trip to Paris finally arrived. Debbie had been counting the days! She felt as childlike as Emma in her impatience. Her work at the hospital had helped to keep her thoughts fully occupied and Emma had needed her. But the thought of two whole days away with Marcel had kept popping into her head.

It hadn't been necessary to involve Francoise in the organisation of her two days away. Emma's friend Céline had been to stay with them for a sleepover and her mother had suggested that Emma go to stay with them one night soon when it would be convenient for Debbie. Debbie had said she had to go away for a couple of days and Céline's mother had agreed she would be happy to have Emma to sleep at their house and would collect and deliver her to school with her own daughter.

On the morning that Debbie was due to set off for Paris she took Emma to the place where the school bus stopped in the village. Emma was excited to be going to stay with Céline, and as soon as her little friend arrived with her mother she made a beeline for her.

'I've packed Emma's pyjamas, toothbrush, clean clothes for tomorrow and so on,' Debbie said, handing over Emma's bag to Sylvie, Céline's mother. 'I hope I haven't forgotten anything.'

'Oh, don't worry,' Sylvie said amiably, jiggling the handle of her baby's pram. 'We're well equipped at home for anything a child could possibly need.'

Debbie leaned over to peep into the pram. Wide blue eyes peered up at her and the baby gave a toothless smile.

'Oh, she's beautiful! And so good!'

'She's good now that I've just fed her. Takes up a lot of my time. I envy you, going out to work. Sometimes I think I'll never escape from the house and have time to myself. But I wouldn't be without my children. Such a blessing, aren't they?'

'Absolutely! It's nice for Céline to have a baby sister.'

'Oh, she adores Marianne! And she's so good with her. I look forward to Céline coming home at the end of the day to play with her. Oh, here's the bus. Céline!'

Emma came up for a hug before running off to climb up the steps to the bus. 'See you tomorrow, Mummy,' she called importantly, before turning to tell the assembled children on the bus that she was going to stay with Céline and wouldn't see her mummy that night.

Debbie swallowed the lump in her throat. Emma was growing up so quickly and soon wouldn't need her quite so much.

'My mobile will be switched on all the time if you need to speak to me, Sylvie,' Debbie said, as she prepared to leave. 'Thank you so much for having her.'

'My pleasure. Have a nice time in Paris!'

As she turned away and began walking back down

the street, Debbie was glad to be leaving Emma with someone like Sylvie who hadn't asked questions about the purpose of her visit to Paris. She probably thought it was something to do with her work at the hospital or else she was going to stay with her father. Or she may have sensed she was meeting a boyfriend and was discreet enough not to enquire. It would have been much more difficult to explain her absence to Francoise, although if she became pregnant she'd have to come clean.

Putting her key in the front door, she decided that she would be completely open with Francoise if or when the time came that she was pregnant. She was going to need Francoise's help if she was to continue working at the hospital before and after the baby was born. One possibility she'd thought of was that Francoise might agree to come and live with them. The extra money Debbie would give her would come in useful and Francoise loved babies.

But as she went back into the empty house and began clearing up the kitchen, she told herself not to count her chickens. Tonight was another step in the right direction. As she thought about it, she felt her body stirring sensually. She was going to spend the whole night with Marcel.

Her mobile rang almost as if on cue. 'Are you ready?'

She suppressed a sigh as she heard his voice. 'Almost.'

'I'll pick you up in half an hour.'

'I'll be ready.'

Debbie put her weekender bag down in the hall as she heard the car pulling into the drive. It had been difficult to decide what to wear, but in the end she'd chosen to travel in her denim trouser suit. And she'd packed her new, floaty chiffon summer dress for the evening. She could wear it again tomorrow during the day if the weather remained hot.

Marcel was getting out of the car as she opened the front door. He came across the drive, his feet crunching on the gravel, smiling broadly. He kissed her lightly on the lips before bending down to pick up her case.

'All set?'

She nodded, suddenly feeling nervous. She'd been looking forward to this day for so long but now it was actually here she wondered if her expectations were too high. Better to calm her excitement and pretend it was simply a day out with Marcel. And a night! At the thought of the night, she remembered that Marcel would be hoping so much that they would create a baby tonight. And so was she.

Marcel was holding open the passenger door for her. She looked up at him and he smiled down at her. He looked relaxed and happy in his casual lightweight suit. He removed his jacket and tossed it into the space behind their seats.

She settled herself in the passenger seat as Marcel started up the engine.

'In two hours we'll be in Paris,' he said as he headed for the autoroute.

As they slowed to take a ticket for the autoroute Marcel glanced sideways and put out a hand to touch her ruffled hair. 'Your hair looks so attractive when the wind ruffles it.'

She laughed. 'I wasted ages brushing it and now it feels like a bird's nest.'

'Leave it like that when you get to Paris. You look like a young girl going out on her first date.'

He handed her the ticket to keep until they got to the *péage* at the end of the motorway before moving swiftly away.

'I feel as if I'm on a first date,' Debbie said, as the car purred along the smooth road. 'I actually think I'm nervous about…well, about everything. Trying for a baby…'

'That wasn't a problem last time, was it?'

She shook her head. 'It was…' She searched for the right words.

'If you enjoyed our night together as much as I did you won't be able to find words to describe it,' he said huskily. 'Just relax, *chérie*. We're going to have a wonderful time in Paris.'

Debbie looked around her as Marcel put their bags on the luggage shelf in the bedroom. She immediately liked the ambience of the room. The décor was predominantly white and typically French. The long windows opened out onto a balcony overlooking the Seine. In spite of the late morning heat outside, the room was cool. She kicked off her shoes and padded out through the window.

'Mmm, what a view!' she said as she admired the gently flowing river, with its pleasure boats and busy launches drifting along in the sunshine. 'It's ages since I went on the river. My father's house is outside Paris and when I go to see him I never have time nowadays to indulge myself. I'd love to take a *bateau mouche* on the river. One like that one over there.'

Marcel came up behind her, putting his arms over her shoulders so that she would lean against him.

'If it's a *bateau mouche* trip you want, *chérie*, that's

what we'll do.' He hesitated. 'You mentioned your father just now. Does he know you're in Paris?'

Debbie shook her head. 'It takes so long to get out to his house. They live near St Germain en Laye. I've promised myself I'll make a special trip soon.'

'That's the other side of Paris from my parents',' Marcel said. 'I haven't told them I'm coming to Paris for the same reason. I feel guilty about it but we need time to ourselves today. We'll make a special journey here as soon as we can tell them about their forthcoming grandchild.'

'Do you think we should tell them as soon as we know? Perhaps we should wait a while. I mean, we're not exactly going to be conventional parents, are we?'

'Your father doesn't sound very conventional to me.' Debbie smiled. 'I suppose not.'

'And my parents are completely unshockable. Besides, we're mature enough to be unconventional if it suits us.'

He took hold of her hand and drew her back into the bedroom. 'Let's go out quickly. If we stay here any longer, I'll be tempted to take you to bed and—'

She laughed. 'Later!'

Debbie was as excited as a young girl as they boarded the *bateau mouche*. She chose to sit on the top deck, enjoying the view as they floated past the spectacular sights she knew so well and yet couldn't admire often enough.

'The Eiffel Tower,' she said, pointing to the huge iron structure. 'My father helped me walk up the iron staircase to the first floor when I was very small. I remember he bought me some chocolate and after he'd pointed out lots of the Paris landmarks he carried me most of the way down again because my legs were aching so much.'

'You don't want to go up the Eiffel Tower today, do you?'

'No, but I'd like to go into Notre Dame. I feel that I'd like to...' She paused. 'I'd like to light a candle.'

After they'd left the *bateau mouche*, they walked along the bank of the river and crossed the bridge to the ancient cathedral. It was cool and quiet inside. Debbie paused to select a candle, putting some money in the box beside them. She lit the candle from the flame burning on the table and made a silent prayer.

Marcel watched her. He instinctively knew this had something to do with their baby and he felt a lump rising in his throat. He hoped it wouldn't be long before her prayers were answered.

They went out into the bright sunshine and walked across the bridge to the left bank of the river. Marcel succeeded in finding a small restaurant where he said he'd had an excellent lunch the last time he'd been in Paris. They chose to sit outside on the pavement, shaded from the sun by a large umbrella.

The waiter placed a carafe of house wine on their table, together with a basket of crusty rolls. Marcel chose oysters for his starter. Debbie decided she would have prawns.

'Oysters are very good for you, *monsieur*,' the waiter said as he gathered up the menus.

Marcel smiled. 'I know.'

After the waiter had gone, Debbie asked Marcel if he believed in the theory that oysters made a man more virile. 'I mean, from a medical point of view, is there any evidence to support the theory?'

Marcel gave her a rakish grin. 'I can feel the magic

working already and the oysters haven't even arrived yet.'

It was late afternoon when they left the restaurant.
They drifted off through the narrow streets back to the
river and crossed to the right bank so that they could
walk up the Champs Élysées. By the time they'd win-
dow-shopped their way to the Arc de Triomphe
Debbie's feet were throbbing with the heat of the pavement.

Marcel hailed a taxi and they returned to their hotel.
The first thing Debbie wanted to do was soak herself in
the huge old-fashioned bath. She emptied scented bath
foam into the water and lay back to relax.

She'd left the door open, hoping that Marcel might
join her. As he came in she looked up at him and smiled
lazily. 'There's room for two,' she said.

'I thought there might be.'

As he stripped off his towelling robe and climbed in,
Debbie felt the last vestige of her nervousness disappear. It felt so natural to be lying here together, their
legs intertwined. Her body had stirred with excitement
as she'd watched Marcel slipping into the water. It was
going to be a fantastic night together. And she wasn't
going to spoil it by thinking about the future implications.

Tonight, as they'd pretended last time, they were lovers intent only on making love with each other. The
outcome, baby or otherwise, wasn't important. What
was important was their love for each other. On her part
she didn't need to pretend. Her love was one hundred
per cent genuine.

And she would pretend that Marcel felt the same
way…just for tonight…

CHAPTER EIGHT

WAKING up in the middle of the night, seeing Marcel sleeping peacefully beside her, Debbie remembered that she'd been determined to pretend he loved her while they'd made love. It hadn't been difficult to imagine that he felt the same way about her as she felt about him. Except, at the end of their love-making, as she'd curled up against him, he'd murmured that she needn't be afraid about the future. He wasn't going to take away her independence.

He'd whispered that even though it was so wonderful for him to have her with him for a whole night, he wouldn't try to change their plan. He knew how important it was to her to remain uncommitted.

Why hadn't she told him how she'd changed radically? There she was, her body tingling with erotic vibes, floating on cloud nine, wanting to stay up there in the clouds for ever... Ah, that was precisely why she hadn't put him wise about how she really felt! Her emotions had been out of control. Marcel was probably in a similar state. And in the emotional turbulence following their love-making she might have drawn him into saying something he would regret. He would feel trapped by a commitment he was trying to avoid.

No, it was far better they stick to the plan they'd made, when their emotions didn't come into the equation. If this was all she could hope for, she would go along with it.

She looked down at Marcel's dark, handsome head,

hair tousled out on the pillow beside her. She knew without a shadow of a doubt that she'd never loved anyone as she loved Marcel.

He stirred in his sleep, opened his eyes and reached out for her. She slid easily into his arms, gazing up at him as if trying to hold onto the memory of his features for the times she would be alone in the future.

'Mmm!' He nuzzled his face into her long dark hair. 'No regrets?'

'About what?'

'About trying for a baby with me?'

She smiled. 'So that's what this was all about, was it? And there was I thinking that maybe...'

He silenced her with a long, lingering kiss. 'I think we ought to make sure, don't you?'

He raised his head to look coaxingly into her eyes. She felt her body yearning to melt into his. He felt hard, erect, yet teasing, taking their love-making slowly this time...caressing her skin, exploring, driving her to distraction before the final ecstatic consummation...

Through the window she could hear the sound of revelry on the river. The bright lights of Paris were illuminating the dark night, reminding her that this was a city that never slept. And neither would she while she could stay awake and make love with Marcel...

Some time during the small hours, Marcel picked up the bedside phone and ordered champagne and smoked salmon sandwiches. The waiter who pushed in the trolley didn't blink an eyelid at the rumpled bed or the couple glowing in the aftermath of making love.

After he'd gone, Marcel raised himself and poured the champagne. Handing a glass to Debbie, he clinked the side of it with his own.

'Here's to our success,' he whispered. 'And if we don't succeed this time, we'll keep going until…'

'Until we're successful.' She hesitated. 'Marcel…'

She took a deep breath. She wanted so much to tell him how she really felt about their plan. How if they'd written it down as a contract on paper she would want to tear it into small pieces and…

'What is it, *chérie*?' He reached forward, caressing the side of her cheek, his eyes full of concern.

No, she had to hold back. She couldn't break up the rapport they had between them by demanding more than he was prepared to give.

She cleared her throat. 'Nothing. Just a little niggling worry about the future.'

He smiled. 'You're always worrying about the future. Take each day as it comes and it will all work out. You'll see.'

She sipped her champagne, telling herself that she would do just that. That was the secret. Take one day at a time and it would all work out easily. That was what she'd believed before she'd fallen in love, but now she knew the problems would always be there.

He reached forward and took her glass from her hand, placing it on the bedside table.

Drawing her against his hard body, he tried to reassure her that what they had between them was all she would ever need. She didn't want to voice her opinion that she knew she wanted their relationship to mean more to both of them.

But that would mean commitment, which she knew was totally out of the question where Marcel was concerned.

They were held up on the autoroute on the way back. A lorry had jackknifed and the police had had to close a large section of the road. After a slow crawl that took nearly four hours Marcel dropped her off at the house, saying that he needed to go to the hospital to check that everything was OK. No, he didn't need her to come in with him. She looked exhausted and should try to get some rest.

Climbing onto her bed, halfway through the afternoon, Debbie set the alarm for an hour ahead. She would wake up so that she could go to meet the school bus in the village. Yes, she did feel exhausted but she wanted very much to be reassured by the sight of her daughter.

Lying back on her bed, her mind became active again, reviewing the memorable events of her time away with Marcel. She would never forget how it had seemed as if they would be together for ever. She'd actively allowed herself to fantasise that their wonderful night was the precursor of many such liaisons. But when she came down to earth from her fantasy world, she knew that was all it was. Pure fantasy. The reality of her world was something quite different, and always would be while the man in her life was the totally uncommitted Marcel.

Emma was delighted to see her as she got off the bus, rushing into Debbie's arms with a whoop of pure happiness. 'Mummy, Mummy, you're back! Sylvie said you might be late and I'd have to go home with her and Céline.'

Sylvie came forward, pushing the pram, smiling at Debbie. 'Did you have a good time in Paris?'

'Most enjoyable. Thank you for looking after Emma.

Perhaps Céline would like to come to stay with us again some time soon?'

Céline said she'd love to. Debbie and Sylvie agreed they'd fix a date over the phone when they had their diaries with them.

All through supper, Emma chattered happily about how she'd helped to look after the baby. She'd helped Sylvie to bathe her before they'd put her in her cot. The cot had a little pink quilt and lacy covers all round the side with tiny rosebuds embroidered on it.

'That's nice,' Debbie said, trying to concentrate on Emma's chatter but her mind still focusing on the events of the previous night and how wonderful it would be if she had her own baby. Wonderful…and yet so complicated.

She decided she needed some mature advice on the subject. Who better than her own father, who'd been through a very similar experience with her mother? Yes, as soon as Emma was asleep she would phone him.

She could hear Emma still enthusing about the baby's pretty bedroom. She really must concentrate and give Emma some feedback.

'The baby's bedroom sounds lovely,' Debbie said. 'And does she have many toys in her room?'

'Oh, lots of dolls and a big doll's house. She can't really play with them herself yet, so Céline and I helped her.' Emma paused, screwing up her little face into an enquiring expression. 'Mummy, there's one thing I don't understand. You know you told me the daddy planted a seed in the mummy to make a baby?'

'Yes, that's correct.' Debbie held her breath.

'Well, how does the daddy actually plant it? I mean, what does he have to…?'

Debbie took a deep breath. 'It's like this. The mummy and daddy lie close to each other and—'

'Sort of cuddling, are they?'

'Yes, it's a very special cuddle that mummies and daddies do.'

'So they must love each other, mustn't they?' Emma looked up at Debbie with innocent blue eyes. 'I mean, if they have to lie close to each other?'

'Yes, they have to love each other,' Debbie said slowly. Everything she was saying was simply reinforcing what she believed—in her own case anyway. She swallowed the lump in her throat before continuing.

'And because they love each other and lie very close, the daddy is able to put the seed that makes the baby in the mummy.'

'Wow! That's really clever! But, Mummy, does it hurt when the daddy puts the seed in the mummy?'

Debbie hesitated. She knew she had to tell her daughter the truth. No more prevarication.

'Actually, darling, it's rather nice.'

'Will I enjoy it when I'm a grown-up mummy and find a daddy to make a baby with?'

'I'm sure you will. Now, have you decided which story you want me to read tonight?'

Debbie spent longer than usual putting Emma to bed, giving her all the attention she craved. But as soon as she was asleep, Debbie remembered her earlier decision to ring her father. He was a wise man, with personal and professional medical experience that would help her sort out her problem.

She went downstairs into the sitting room, curled up on the sofa with a cup of coffee and dialled André Sabatier's mobile number. This was going to be a private conversation and she didn't want the whole of his household listening in.

'*Papa, c'est* Debbie.'

She spoke French with her father most of the time because her French was better than his English. In her younger days when he'd come over to England often, he'd been totally fluent. But now retired, André rarely needed to speak English except occasionally to his daughter and granddaughter.

'*Ah,* Debbie! *Comment ca va?*'

She told her father she was very well and asked how he was. He said the arthritis in his hip was still troubling him but he was playing tennis as much as he could so he didn't get stiff.

She'd never thought of her father as ever being anything but a young active man but he was now in his mid-sixties, although he didn't look it. The thought that his health wasn't good increased the guilt she'd been feeling at not visiting him while she'd been in Paris.

'I'm sorry to hear your arthritis is worse. Have you got a good orthopaedic consultant?'

'The best! He was a student of mine for a time when he was a youngster and thinking of specialising in general surgery. I keep him on his toes now, always asking awkward questions about what he's going to do with me.' André gave a little laugh before clearing his throat. 'So what's the news at your end, Debbie? Still enjoying your work in Urgences? What's the hospital at St Martin sur mer like? I've never been there. One of the purpose-built newer hospitals, isn't it?'

'Yes. It's a good hospital to work in. Excellent facilities. I've actually had a couple of days off.' She paused. 'Papa, I've been to Paris but I didn't have time to come out to see you and Louise while I was there.'

'That's perfectly all right, my dear. I know you're very busy. Was your visit to Paris something to do with your work at the hospital?'

'Not exactly…in fact, not at all! I was actually with a colleague, a male colleague. I'm very fond of him…' Her voice trailed away as she realised she didn't know how she was going to explain the situation.

'I see,' her father said in an easy tone. 'Sounds to me like you're more than fond of this man.'

'What makes you say that?'

She heard her father laughing on the end of the line. 'You forget I'm an expert diagnostician. From the sound of your breathy, excited voice I would say you were suffering from an acute or even chronic case of being in love. I'm intrigued. Do you want to tell me some more about your new boyfriend? Will I like him?'

She took a deep breath. 'I'm sure you would like him if you met him professionally. His name is Marcel De Lange and—'

'Yes, I know the man you mean. I met him at a conference once where I was speaking. He gave an excellent paper on…can't remember what at the moment. My memory isn't what it used to be. He was talking about some aspect of surgery he was keen to improve. He's working here in Paris at—'

'No, he's moved. He's working at the St Martin hospital as consultant in charge of Urgences. I'm sure you'll like him when—I mean if you meet him.' She hesitated. 'But there's a problem. You see…'

'He's not married, is he? He didn't have a wife with him when he was at the conference.'

'No, he's divorced, like me. And because we've both had such a terrible time with our previous partners, neither of us wants a committed relationship…but we would both like a baby. We thought that we might be able to find a solution to the problem if we got together.'

She'd spoken hurriedly in a matter-of-fact tone, as if the situation was perfectly natural.

There was silence at the other end as her father digested this information.

'*Papa, tu es toujours là?* Are you still there?'

'Yes, I'm still here, but I'm a bit confused. So you're planning to try for a baby together? Is that what you're leading up to, Debbie?'

'Yes, only it's not as simple as that…'

'Simple! Whoever said it was simple? Producing a child is certainly not simple.'

She drew in her breath. Her father's tone showed his disapproval.

'Well, it would be considerably simpler if I hadn't fallen in love with Marcel. That's the real problem. You see, when we decided we wanted to have a child together, neither of us wanted to make a commitment to a full-time relationship. We agreed that we'd do everything we could to give the child a good start in life but keep our own independent lives intact.'

'Ah! And now you want to change the rules, is that it?'

'Afraid so.'

A long pause. Debbie waited to hear if her father had any advice on this delicate situation. She waited. Eventually she heard him drawing in his breath, swirling a drink that had ice cubes in it. She could picture him now sunk deeply into the leather chair in his study, his brow furrowed as he gave all his attention to his daughter's problems, as he always had done.

'And how does Marcel feel about this?'

'That's the problem. I daren't tell him. I don't want to spoil the rapport we have between us. He wants to keep his freedom. He's such an independent sort of man and we both promised—'

'Debbie you're heading for trouble,' her father said quietly.

She felt a cold shiver running down her spine. 'But you and Mum managed to keep your independence and give me all the love I needed. You were always there for me, always...'

She was holding back tears now. How could her father say she was heading for trouble when he'd been through a similar experience? She'd phoned up for reassurance, not to be told that...

'I agree that both your mother and I gave you all the love you needed. But whereas your mother was adamant that she didn't want a committed relationship with me, I wanted everything with her. I wanted marriage, more children, a life devoted to each other. I wanted to show her all the love I felt for her but...'

He broke off and she heard him sighing deeply. 'I'm over it now because eventually I found Louise.' He lowered his voice. 'But it was your mother who was always the love of my life. She broke my heart and it was impossible to mend.'

Debbie swallowed hard. 'I had no idea! I mean, I knew that Mum was totally focused on her career but...' She broke off, feeling a great surge of pity for the strong, indomitable man who'd always been there for her, never realising how he'd suffered in the process.

'Debbie, don't go down that road. Pull out of this arrangement you've made with Marcel. He'll break your heart if you don't.'

'Papa, I'm too heavily committed.'

André drew in his breath. 'Are you already pregnant?'

'I may be.'

'If you're not pregnant, my advice is to give up the idea of having another child unless you're with someone who's going to live with you and love you for the rest of your life. I'm sorry I sound so negative, but my advice comes from bitter experience.'

'I can see that,' Debbie said quietly.

'Let me know…how things develop, won't you?'

'Of course. And thanks, Dad, for your advice.'

'I doubt you'll take it,' he said lightly. 'You'll probably decide to suffer as I did. But I sincerely hope you'll think long and hard about what you're taking on. A child is for life, and both parents need to be committed to the child…and to each other. My strongest piece of advice is to cool this relationship as soon as you can. And unless you find that you're pregnant, make a clean break and a fresh start.'

Her father hung up and Debbie cradled the phone in her hand for a few seconds, feeling terribly vulnerable. What had she taken on? The awful thing was that she wasn't sure that having another baby was worth paying the price of suffering like her father had done.

During the next couple of weeks at the hospital, she tried to remain as emotionally detached as possible from Marcel. But it was so difficult! They had to work together and being physically close as they struggled to save a patient's life or conferred about a difficult case was not conducive to cool, impersonal behaviour.

She saw the puzzled expression in Marcel's eyes when on a couple of occasions she said she couldn't go out with him that evening. She knew he wasn't fooled but was making the point that he had no hold on her. He respected her independence to live her own life.

Late one afternoon, as she was about to go off duty an unconscious patient was brought in. A witness testified that she'd seen a young woman falling from a car on the autoroute. Then another witness who'd been in a car close behind said they'd noticed the driver and the woman having an obviously heated argument. Shortly before the woman had fallen from the car, the driver had hit the woman. The door had then opened and the woman had fallen out before the driver had continued to leave the scene at speed.

The second witness was prepared to swear on oath that the driver had pushed the now badly injured woman out. Everything hinged on whether the woman could be revived to tell exactly what happened.

Marcel was dealing with another patient who'd sustained relatively minor burns when trying to put out a fire in the storeroom of the shop where he was working. Urgences was now swarming with policemen intent on getting at the truth. Marcel paged Debbie, asking her if she could take over his burns case. He needed to deal with the police and restore some order in Urgences so that his staff could concentrate on treating the unconscious woman.

'I don't like to ask you when you're supposed to be on your way home, but this is a real emergency and we're short-staffed this afternoon.'

'No problem,' Debbie said briskly. 'Francoise is collecting Emma.'

She hurried to the treatment room where Marcel had been treating the burns case. Marie was treating the burns on the patient's arms.

'First-degree burns,' she whispered. 'He's been very

lucky. Marcel has contacted the burns unit and we've got one of the team arriving shortly to take over.'

For a few minutes, Debbie helped with the preliminary treatment until the burns specialist arrived. As soon as she'd handed over she went to check on how Marcel was coping with the new emergency.

It was long past the time she should have gone off duty, but Urgences was still in a chaotic state. The press had now arrived and nobody seemed to be dealing with them. She found Marcel bending over his unconscious patient, shining a bright light into her eyes as he checked for her ophthalmic reaction. He looked up and smiled with relief as Debbie arrived.

'I've dealt with the police but now the press are asking for a statement. Apparently, the second witness is making a great fuss about what he saw. At this stage, whether she fell or whether she was pushed is of no interest to me. I'm a doctor, trying to save a patient's life. Will you deal with the press for me?'

'Of course.'

Debbie went out into the main reception area. The vociferous witness who had claimed that their patient had been pushed from the car was surrounded by several journalists, all keen to get a story.

Debbie moved into the middle of the crowd, politely requesting that they all leave as soon as possible.

'We have no further information to give you,' she said firmly. 'Later, when we have had time to assess the situation, a hospital spokesman will give you more details. But for the moment our only concern is that we should take care of our patients here in Urgences.'

'It's all gone quiet again out there,' Marcel said, looking up from his patient as Debbie returned to the cubicle where he was working. 'What did you do? Anaesthetise everybody?'

'They all went quietly. I think they thought I was more important than I am.'

'Oh, but you're very important, Debbie.' He lowered his voice. 'Especially to me.'

There was not as much as a flicker of an eyelid from the young houseman helping Marcel. But Debbie noticed that the two nurses who'd been assigned the job of handing over the instruments from the trolley were smiling with interest. The hospital grapevine had already picked up on the fact that she and Marcel had been seeing each other. She could tell that everyone was interested in where their relationship was heading.

If they only knew!

Marcel straightened up so that he could focus on what the CT scan had revealed. 'I'm going to transfer our patient to Theatre. It's essential that we relieve the intracranial pressure.'

Debbie looked across at the CT scan that Marcel was studying.

Marcel pointed to the trouble spot. 'See that great dark mass at the base of the skull?'

Debbie nodded. 'That looks like a sizeable haematoma, doesn't it?'

'Exactly!' Marcel peeled off his gloves.

The phone rang. 'It's the brain consultant, wanting to speak to you from Theatre,' one of the nurses said.

Marcel took the call. 'Fine. You're ready now? Yes, I'd like to be there. I agree, it's a complicated case.'

A junior doctor had arrived with a theatre nurse. The unconscious patient was carefully transferred to the trolley.

Debbie went out into the corridor. Marcel hurried after her. 'Thanks for staying on, Debbie.'

'Glad to be of help,' she said lightly.

He put his hand on her arm. 'Is everything OK with you?'

'Of course. Why do you ask?'

'Well, you've seemed a bit distant recently. Ever since we went to Paris you seem as if you're avoiding me.'

'Marcel!' Marie called. 'You're needed in Theatre.'

'I'm coming.' He leaned forward. 'We need to talk about…about whatever's worrying you.'

'We will,' she said quietly.

As soon as she began walking away from him she knew they would have to talk about how she was now feeling. Since her father had given her his advice to cool her relationship with Marcel, she'd been thrown into emotional confusion. Her head was telling her to take her father's advice. He'd been in the same situation and had suffered for the rest of his life because of his unrequited love for her mother. But her heart was telling her that because she loved Marcel she was prepared to suffer the hard times for the sake of the happy times in between.

As she walked down the corridor she reflected on what was uppermost in her mind at the moment. Her period was late. She would wait a few more days and then use the pregnancy kit she'd bought. And if she was pregnant, how was she going to deal with it? She should be overjoyed, but the initial scenario had changed. She'd changed so much since she and Marcel had first got together.

If only she could say the same for Marcel!

CHAPTER NINE

DEBBIE experienced feelings of extreme happiness mixed with alarm as she stared at the thin blue line. She'd half expected she would get a positive reaction with her pregnancy kit. When she'd first climbed out of bed this morning she'd felt decidedly queasy. A bit early in her pregnancy for that, but then she'd remembered how she'd felt for the first few months with Emma.

At the time she'd put some of her discomfort down to the fact that she'd had to contend with Paul moaning that he didn't think they could afford a baby. He'd asked her why she hadn't taken more care, insinuating that it had been all her fault.

It didn't seem to occur to Paul that he'd had anything to do with the conception. She'd had tonsillitis at the time and the antibiotics she'd been taking must have cancelled out the Pill. But she'd been thrilled when Emma had been born. She'd never for one second regretted having her daughter, though even with two salaries coming in, they had always seemed hard up. Paul had always been deliberately vague so, loving him unreservedly as she had, she hadn't realised at that point that he'd had a mistress.

She sat down on the stool in her bathroom and put her head in her hands as the unpleasant memories came flooding back. She'd thought that this time she would have been over the moon at the prospect of a much-wanted child, but the prospect of bringing up the child without Marcel there all the time suddenly seemed very daunting.

Her father's words had struck fear into her heart. He'd always kept up the pretence that all had been well when he'd visited them in London. But, looking back, she remembered her mother's cool manner on occasions. She'd always thought it had been because her mother had never had enough time to spend on the occasions when André had been in London.

Now that he'd explained the full story, it all fell into place. Her mother had been very focused on her career as a successful surgeon, one of few women to scale the heights that she had. But she'd also had fun in her private life, something which Debbie had accepted. Actually, she'd put it at the back of her mind and forgotten about it entirely!

Until her father had spoken about his broken heart. And now she'd got herself into exactly the same position. She mustn't be lulled into the idea that because she was the mother of Marcel's adored child he would feel under any obligation to be faithful to her. Her heart would be broken time after time in the future if she didn't pull herself together and hold onto her emotions.

Marcel was a handsome, sexy man who would undoubtedly have many girlfriends over the coming years. Their commitment to each other was to produce a child and go their separate independent ways. Marcel had said he wouldn't commit to any woman ever again. But that didn't preclude making love with women who were simply looking for a romantic liaison.

How naïve she had been when she'd agreed to try for a baby with Marcel! But love changed everything. Not necessarily for the better in her case.

She sat up and reached for a towel as she told herself

to snap out of it. She shouldn't have deliberately tried for a baby if she'd had doubts about it. But she'd had few doubts at the beginning of her big adventure with Marcel. It will all work out, he'd told her constantly. Think positively. Yes, that was what she had to do. Concentrate on the main fact, that it would be wonderful to have another child in the house. A sister or brother for Emma.

She stepped into her shower cubicle and turned the taps full on. As the water cascaded down over her shoulders she told herself that her little family would be complete...wouldn't it? This was all she'd ever wanted...wasn't it?

As she got dressed she decided that she would wait until she was about three months pregnant before she told Emma, make sure the pregnancy was fully established. The first three months was the period when most miscarriages occurred and she would hate to disappoint Emma.

But she would have to tell Marcel soon. She gathered up some discarded clothes and ran with them downstairs to load the washing machine. For the first time in her life she felt she would like to stay at home and have a completely domestic day. Spend her time mopping the kitchen floor, doing some ironing. Anything but talk to Marcel about the pregnancy.

OK, she told herself. A bit of early morning domestic stuff and then off to the hospital. First priority after the domestic bit...tell Marcel soon.

Soon as in that morning!

The reception area of Urgences was relatively quiet when she arrived. The staff were going about their routine tasks. It was still early in the day. The overnight emergencies had been treated and discharged or admitted. Time for the next set of emergencies to begin.

She asked Marie if Marcel was there yet. Marie said he was in his office. Debbie went along the corridor and tapped lightly on the door.

'Entrez!'

She took a deep breath, pushed open the door and walked purposefully across the carpet towards Marcel's desk.

Marcel looked up and smiled, pushing away the papers he was working on as he rose to his feet.

She took another deep breath. It would feel more natural if she told Marcel the news in English.

'Marcel, I've done a test this morning. I'm pregnant.'

'Qu'est-ce que tu as dit? What did you say?' Marcel ran round the desk to enfold her in his arms. 'Oh, Debbie, how wonderful! Come and sit down. We've got to make plans. I was hoping…I was praying… But now we need to make plans.'

Debbie smiled as she felt her tense body relaxing. Marcel's boyish enthusiasm was just what she needed to boost her morale.

'Hold on a moment, Marcel. We've got plenty of time. The baby's not due until next May. I'm going to carry on working as long as possible and—'

'Oh, no, you're not! I decided that when you fell pregnant I would arrange for the appointment of another doctor to replace you for at least the last three months of your pregnancy. It's better for you and the baby if you stop work, let's say in…January. That will give you plenty of time to prepare and—'

'Marcel!'

Debbie reached across and touched his arm. He was bending over her chair, his eyes shining with happiness.

This was the moment she'd longed for. The moment when she told Marcel that he was going to be a father. She didn't want to spoil the magic moment for him. Nothing had changed for him. This was all he'd wanted. To become a father. He was having no difficulty with accepting their original plan.

But her own feelings were now more complicated. She had to reaffirm her independence if she was going to save herself from having to mend her broken heart.

'Marcel, I'd like to be in charge of my pregnancy,' she said quietly. 'I'd like to organise my work schedule to suit me.'

He stared at her. 'It's your pregnancy but it's our baby, remember. I want only the best for the baby. And I don't want you to get tired so I'll set the wheels in motion so that we interview some doctors. We need another doctor who can speak good English. Your English has been so useful recently when we've had English tourists requiring treatment.'

He walked across to the window, pulling up the Venetian blinds so that the sun came streaming in.

'Oh, Debbie. I'm so happy! You've made me the happiest man in the world. I want to go around and shout the good news to everybody I meet.'

He turned round to face her again, his face radiant. 'I'm going to be a father! I'm going to—'

'Please, Marcel, let's keep it quiet for a while,' she said gently. 'I mean, it's early days and something might happen. You know as well as I do that from a medical point of view, until the pregnancy is firmly established it's better that…'

He walked back across the room and drew her gently to her feet, holding her tenderly as if she was very precious to him.

'Nothing is likely to happen, as you put it,' he said quietly. He hesitated, looking down at her with a quizzical expression. 'Is it that you simply don't want to announce the fact that you're having a baby with me?'

She looked up into his eyes and felt her body stirring with desire. But she was trying to remain focused on what she had to say. She had to establish the way that their relationship was to develop in the future, given that she wanted to limit the damage to her already bruised heart.

'Marcel, I'm going to tell everybody you're the father of my baby…but not yet. Give me a few weeks to think out what I'm going to say. I mean, it's not as if this was a conventional pregnancy, is it?'

He sighed. 'No, it's not. Is that what's been worrying you ever since we got back from Paris? You've been so quiet with me. Not at all like your usual self.'

She pulled herself away from his embrace so that she could think clearly. Whenever she was close to him it was difficult to remain objective.

'I've been feeling a bit queasy, that's all,' she said, hating herself for telling a white lie. It was half-true anyway. She had been feeling queasy. 'Now that I know for certain I'm pregnant, I'll be able to cope better.'

She lowered her voice, looking away so that she didn't have to watch the perplexed expression on his face. 'But, please, don't crowd me.'

He looked alarmed. 'Crowd you? What do you mean?'

She began again, in French this time. 'I need space. I need to come to terms with what's happening to my changing body…and to my changing life.'

Marcel took a step forward but seemed to check himself from reaching out towards her.

'Of course you need space, *chérie*,' he said. 'I shall respect your desire to remain independent even though you're carrying my child. So I'll contain my excitement and keep our secret for the first few weeks.'

'When my waistline starts to thicken at around four months, we'll make an announcement together but until then…'

'Four months! You want me to keep this to myself for four months? *C'est impossible, chérie!*'

'No it's not impossible. Please, Marcel.'

She knew she was playing for time. Time to come to terms with this new situation. The situation that they'd created and agreed on. But a situation that now filled her with apprehension about the future. Yes, she was thrilled that she was going to have another baby. She already loved the tiny life growing inside her.

But she couldn't help wishing that she and Marcel were fully committed to each other. That was never going to happen so she had to keep herself from being hurt too much and too often…as her father had been.

During the days that followed Marcel kept his promise not to reveal their news to anyone. They saw each other in their off-duty hours whenever they could. There was a small concert hall in the middle of St Martin sur mer, and Marcel was a member of the subscription ticket club. He asked Debbie to go with him on several occasions and she enjoyed the intimate atmosphere of the chamber music concerts.

The standard of playing by the instrumentalists was first class because good musicians came from other regions of France to supplement the long list of enthusiastic local players. She found herself looking forward to each concert she attended with him. And she enjoyed having supper with him afterwards in one of the small restaurants close by. The initial weeks of her pregnancy were passing by more easily than she'd anticipated on that first morning when she'd done the pregnancy test.

One evening, when she was three months pregnant, a string quartet came down from Paris and played music by Haydn and Brahms. As the haunting music of the strings wafted over her, she turned to glance at Marcel. He was looking so handsome this evening. His happiness at being a prospective father was palpable. Some of their colleagues had remarked on how well he looked during the last few weeks but he'd contained his secret with admirable restraint.

As if sensing she was looking at him, he turned towards her, smiled and reached for her hand. She felt a frisson of desire ripple through her. She knew that Marcel had wanted to make love with her during the past few weeks. Several times recently when they'd said goodnight, he'd held her very close. But she knew he'd been holding himself back because she'd indicated that she wanted to play safe in the crucial early stages of her pregnancy.

Tonight, she decided, if Marcel lingered over their goodnight kiss she would make it obvious that she still desired him. She could allow a little romance to creep into their relationship now and again if that was what they both wanted. In the future, when Marcel moved away from her, it wouldn't be so easy for her. She wouldn't be so sure that he wanted to make love with her. But now, when she knew it was what he wanted, she was determined to go for it.

She had no idea if Marcel had been seeing any other women during the past few weeks. That was one idea she would have to accept if she was to survive emotionally in the future.

She'd had no reason to suspect him of seeing someone else. She couldn't bear to think about it and banished it from her mind whenever the awful thought cropped up!

Going out into the cool evening after the concert, Marcel put an arm around her waist as he guided her to the car park.

'I thought it was a very good concert tonight,' he said, as he held open the passenger door for her. 'What did you think of it?'

Debbie smiled. 'I enjoyed it very much. I thought the first violinist was exceptionally good.'

'So did I. He's with us again in a week's time, playing the Bach violin concerto in A minor. If you're free that evening, I've got a couple of tickets.'

'Thank you. I'd love to come.'

Marcel started the engine. 'Which restaurant would you like to go to tonight? I phoned Au Bon Acceuil and they only had tables early in the evening. We could go to—'

'If you've got some eggs, I could make an omelette back at your place. I feel like relaxing tonight in a place where I can take my shoes off and loosen my belt.'

'What a good idea!'

Marcel drove out through the gates of the car park, looking each way before driving onto the seafront road.

'Except I'll make the omelette while you put your feet up and watch me, Debbie. No, I insist! You've been on your feet all day.'

In the kitchen, ensconced in the armchair near the cooker, Debbie felt cosseted as she sipped her glass of orange juice. This was the sort of intimacy she craved now that she was carrying Marcel's child. A family atmosphere. Whenever she managed to arrange this cosy kind of ambience in the future, she would savour every moment of the experience as she was doing now.

She was heading for heartbreak, allowing herself to get carried away as she intended to tonight, but she would hold back later! For one night she wanted to imagine that they were a real family. Emma had been invited to another sleepover at the house of one of her friends from school.

She hadn't yet told Marcel that she'd like to stay the night. She wouldn't blame him if he turned her down! He'd probably given up on her because of the way she'd tried to cool down their relationship. She'd better play it by ear, make sure it was what they both wanted. It wasn't too late to drive home.

Marcel was whisking the eggs now. He looked up and smiled at her.

'So you had to loosen your belt, did you? That's exciting news! I remember you said that when your waist thickened we would announce our secret to the world and in particular to our medical colleagues.'

Debbie smiled. 'My waist hasn't really thickened yet. It's pure imagination on my part. But my belt felt uncomfortable during the concert. I remember saying that it would thicken around four months. When baby begins to show, we'll make our announcement.'

Marcel tossed a sizeable slab of butter into the omelette pan and took a sip from his glass of wine as he waited for it to sizzle.

'Have you arranged to have a three-month scan?'

She hesitated, hoping that Marcel wouldn't suggest he would like to go with her.

'Actually, I've arranged to go tomorrow. I'll have a photograph taken and bring it to show you,' she added quickly.

Marcel put the whisked eggs into the prepared pan. 'I should hope you will.'

She felt relieved that he hadn't asked to come with her. It was impossible not to admire the way he'd stuck to his promise and allowed her to go it alone for these first few weeks. But she had no idea how he would behave when she was four months pregnant and their secret came out.

'That omelette was delicious!' Debbie said as she helped herself to salad from the large wooden bowl on the kitchen table.

'I'll drive you home tonight, Debbie,' Marcel said. 'I don't like the idea of you driving so late by yourself. If something happened to you on the way home…'

'Actually, Marcel, I'd like to stay the night if that's OK with you. Emma's away for the night with friends.'

Marcel's eyes flickered but his enigmatic expression didn't change. 'My *femme de ménage* always keeps the guest room ready. I'll make sure there's a dressing-gown in there for you when you go upstairs.'

Her frustration mounted. Well, she couldn't blame Marcel for interpreting her wishes in that way. He'd obviously come to terms with the cooler atmosphere in their relationship.

'Thank you,' she said politely, feeling a cold chill settling around her heart. She would have to get used to this sort of ambivalent situation in the future.

Looking across the table, she saw that Marcel was

smiling, his sexy lips parted as he studied her enquiringly. It was almost as if he was reading her thoughts. With swift fluid movements he rose to his feet and came round the table, putting his hands on her shoulders.

'Alternatively, you could share my bed,' he said huskily. 'It's a big bed and you won't even know I'm there...unless you invite me over to your side for a goodnight kiss or...'

'Marcel, I want you to hold me close tonight,' she whispered, looking up at him with a shy smile. 'I feel so...'

She checked herself before she could reveal her true feelings. He must never know how vulnerable she felt. She must continue to pretend that she loved her independence, her lack of commitment to him. Otherwise she would lose him completely and there would be no more romantic liaisons. If she could learn to enjoy the brief times of happiness she spent with Marcel, she wouldn't suffer as much from unrequited love as her father had done.

He held out his hand and drew her to her feet before holding her close. Gently he bent down and lifted her into his arms.

'You won't be able to do that much longer,' she joked as he carried her out through the kitchen door.

'You're still as light as a feather,' he whispered as he began to mount the stairs. 'I'm going to be very gentle with you tonight, Debbie, simply hold you in my arms, but...'

'Please, darling, let's make love.'

She looked up at him as he carried her up the stairs, wondering how she could so easily dismiss the small voice in her head that was telling her to get a grip on her emotions. Make love, yes, but don't lose your heart to him... Impossible! But would she think it was worth the inevitable heartache for one more heavenly night with Marcel?

He paused as they reached the bend in the staircase, lowering his head so that he could kiss her on the lips. She parted her lips, savouring the moment, intent on remembering this night for the rest of her life. It would be a long time before she allowed herself another night of bliss like this...

Waking up in Marcel's bed, Debbie stretched herself, feeling as lithe and supple as a kitten. It had been a totally different experience, making love with Marcel last night. She had never known such tenderness before... and yet the passion had still been there. He'd simply been so touchingly careful when he'd caressed her. And when he'd moved inside her he'd seemed conscious that he mustn't harm the baby. Their bodies had moved together as if performing a slow, leisurely, rhythmical dance.

As she'd given herself up to the steady rhythm it had seemed to Debbie a celebration of her pregnancy. As their bodies had fused, she'd felt the pace of the rhythm increasing and when the climax had come she'd called out Marcel's name, clutching his back so hard that she felt she may have bruised him.

She hadn't wanted him to leave her body. She'd wanted to stay like that, fused together, as if they would never be apart.

So different from reality! She watched Marcel as he stirred now in his sleep. It was time to tiptoe away. She didn't want to be here when he woke up. She couldn't bear to repeat the experience. Last night she'd allowed herself to imagine that they were a real family. Today she had to come back down to earth.

Quietly she followed the trail of her discarded clothes, picking up garments as she went out onto the landing.

'Debbie, what are you doing?'

As she heard Marcel's sleepy voice, she sighed. Too late! She poked her head round the bedroom door. 'I've got to get back home. I want to change my clothes and pick up some things I need for the scan this morning.'

'But it's so early. It's still dark. Come back to bed and I'll bring you a hot drink and something to eat. You shouldn't go out on an empty stomach in your condition.'

She went back across the room and leaned down to kiss Marcel's cheek. He looked so utterly desirable with his rumpled hair and little-boy expression as he rubbed his eyes.

'I have to go,' she said firmly.

Marcel groaned. 'I shall never understand you. Perhaps that's part of the fascination. You're such an enigma.'

He put out a hand to detain her, but she evaded his grasp. As she made for the door she was thinking that it was good to know he found her fascinating. But fascination would never be enough for him to make a life-long commitment to her.

'Don't forget to have a photo made of our baby,' he called as she went out onto the landing.

'I promise.'

She hurried down the stairs, anxious to be out of the house before she could change her mind and go back to snuggle up beside Marcel again.

Her body was still tingling with the aftermath of their

love-making. It had been a heavenly experience, spending the night with Marcel again. She had no regrets about letting down her guard. She planned to do this from time to time in the future—when she felt that it was what Marcel wanted, too.

But now it was time to listen to the rational sensible small voice in her head and stop following her heart. It seemed simple to her now that their romance should continue for as long as Marcel still wanted her. But she was storing up heartache for the future. Sooner or later he would tire of being part-time lover to the mother of his child.

And that was when he would cool their relationship—as her mother had done with her father—and Debbie knew her heart would break...

CHAPTER TEN

As SHE lay on the examination couch, waiting for the scan to begin, Debbie looked up at the white ceiling above her, feeling decidedly nervous. She tried to focus on one spot on the ceiling. There was a hook with a light hanging down. There was no bulb in the light socket. She wondered why. She closed her eyes. Trying to distract herself by concentrating on her surroundings didn't help.

She'd scanned many pregnant women during her training in obstetrics but it was quite a different prospect when she was the patient. She was longing to see the fuzzy images of her baby on the monitor, but at the same time she was apprehensive.

She wanted her baby to be perfect in every way, for her own as well as for Marcel's sake. Having witnessed a full range of pregnancy complications during her medical training and work as a doctor, the slightest perceived abnormality that appeared on the screen would make her active brain go into overdrive.

'Madame Sabatier?'

A kindly middle-aged motherly-looking nurse came in and smiled down at her. *'Vous êtes prête, madame?'*

Debbie smiled back and said, yes, she was quite ready. As she watched the nurse massaging the greasy scanning cream over her abdomen she knew she was glad to have chosen a private obstetric clinic away from the hospital. It would have been impossible to keep the grapevine tongues from wagging if she'd simply gone along to the hospital obstetric department.

The clinic she'd chosen was several kilometres from the hospital, set in lovely, well-kept grounds, inland from St Martin sur mer. It was an old château that had been converted into a fully equipped obstetric and gynaecological clinic.

Her medical consultant had been utterly discreet when she'd first gone to see him. She'd told him that she was a single mother and this was her second child. He'd examined her and pronounced her in good health. He had asked if the father of the baby was healthy and she'd said he was. That was the only time the father had been mentioned. And she hadn't even told him she was a doctor.

At that point it hadn't seemed relevant and she'd been intent on keeping her anonymity. News travelled fast in medical circles!

A medical technician was switching on the screen. Debbie could feel the nurse moving the scanner over her abdomen. She focused her eyes on the screen set to one side of the examination couch.

'There, I can see him...or her!' she cried out excitedly.

The nurse turned her head to look at the screen as she continued to move the scanner over Debbie's abdomen.

'Do you want to know the sex of your baby, Madame Sabatier?'

'Yes, I think I do.'

'And the father, does he want to know?'

Debbie had no idea. It wasn't something they'd discussed. 'Probably,' she said vaguely. 'The image on the screen is very small. It's not always possible to discern the sex with a scan at three months, is it?'

'Sometimes it's possible,' the nurse said. 'If not, we can run the test on you afterwards to determine the sex of your baby.'

'There! Look just there, Nurse! I'm sure that's a boy, don't you think?'

The nurse smiled. 'I think you're right, but we'll run a test at the end to make sure. Were you hoping for a boy?'

Debbie smiled back. 'I'm just hoping for a healthy child. My daughter wants a baby sister but if it really is a boy I know she'll still be thrilled.'

'What did your daughter say when you told her you were pregnant?'

'I haven't told her yet.' Debbie hesitated. 'You know, first three months, wanting to make sure that everything's OK before...'

'Oh, you must tell her soon! Let her share in the excitement and wonder of Mummy having a baby. You've got a healthy baby and your own health is excellent, according to your case notes. I've got four children and each new baby was a wonderful shared experience for the others.'

'I'm sure it was. I'll tell her soon. Are you going to take a photo of my baby?'

'Of course! It's standard practice here. Your daughter will want to see it...and the baby's father, I expect.'

Driving along the road to St Martin, Debbie reflected on her morning as a patient. It had been a strange experience. She'd felt so vulnerable when she'd been in the hands of the capable nurse. She would have to let go and learn to trust again. Listen to advice from those who'd been through more childbirth experiences than herself. She was never going to have a cosy family unit, mother, father and children all in the same house, but she could make her unconventional family as happy as possible…under the circumstances.

She took one hand off the steering-wheel to touch her bag on the passenger seat. She'd got three pictures of her son. The test had confirmed she was carrying a boy. One copy for Emma, one copy for herself and one copy for Marcel.

She was nearing the village now. She'd taken the whole day off duty so had the whole of the afternoon to herself. Bliss! She went into the house, poured a glass of milk from the fridge, kicked off her shoes and lay down on the sofa.

Her mobile phone rang. She cursed silently as she reached into the depths of her bag.

'How did it go?' Marcel asked in English.

She smiled. 'The baby's fine. He's fine.'

'He?'

'Yes, I thought I could see he was a boy on the screen. It was a bit fuzzy so they tested me to make sure.'

'That's wonderful! And everything is OK with you?'

'I was pronounced perfectly fit.'

'Have you got a photo of the scan?'

'I've got three—one for you, one for me and one for Emma.'

'When will you give it to her?'

Debbie hesitated. 'I was going to wait another month until I started showing but maybe I'll tell her about the baby this evening. When I've finally decided how I'm going to explain the situation. She's only six but—'

'Would you like me to come over and help you out

with all the inevitable questions? You'll have to tell her I'm the father, won't you?'

Again she hesitated before relief flooded through her. The explanation would be complicated but with Marcel's help it would be easier.

'Yes, I think we're agreed you'd be with me when I tell Emma.'

'Why do you sound so apprehensive? Emma will be thrilled to know she's going to have a baby brother.'

Debbie sighed. 'I know. It's explaining that you're the father that's the difficult bit.' She paused. 'I believe I told you she doesn't want anyone to replace her own father.'

'I've no intention of trying to take his place! Emma's probably realised that by now. We get on very well when we see each other.'

'I know you do. But also Emma's idea of how babies are conceived is still a bit sketchy. I gave her a true version that a six-year-old would understand but there are gaps in her knowledge that could be a bit tricky.'

'Oh, don't worry about it. It's not rocket science, is it? She's an intelligent six-year-old. She'll be able to understand what happened.'

That's what I'm afraid of! Debbie thought anxiously. 'We'll see what she makes of it when we talk this evening.'

'I'll finish early if possible. *A tout à l'heure*, see you soon.'

She lay back against the cushions, her hands clasped over her abdomen. Yes, her tummy did feel a bit more rounded already. Well, her dear little baby boy was swimming around in his own private pool, getting bigger every day. She felt drowsy. She gave in as her eyelids drooped, falling quickly into a deep sleep.

*   *   *

It was late when she woke up. She glanced at the sitting-room clock. Only minutes now to get to the bus stop in the village and meet Emma! She'd told Francoise she would collect her today as she had a day off.

Jumping up, she reached for her warm jacket, which was still on a chair where she'd flung it when she'd come in. Hurrying out of the house, she slammed the door shut before checking for her keys.

Relief! The keys were in her jacket pocket. She was barely awake yet and it was difficult to concentrate. Thoughts about the baby were running through her head, mixed with thoughts about Marcel.

He was coming to see her this evening. That bit she remembered clearly. She turned up the hood of her jacket as a thin drizzle began. The sky was already becoming dark as the clouds loomed overhead.

Tonight was the big night when she would tell Emma about the coming baby, when she would have to explain somehow that Marcel was the baby's father. Her sharp-witted daughter with the ever-enquiring mind wouldn't let her off lightly about that situation! What she would make of it, Debbie had no idea.

There she was, already stepping off the bus with a purposeful step. For an instant Emma reminded Debbie of her mother. The long blonde hair, the determined self-confidence. Emma would need to be given all the facts this evening and the questions would be endless.

'Emma!'

'Mummy!' As she ran towards her Debbie realised she was still an innocent child. She would be receptive to everything that Debbie told her this evening. It was a big responsibility to teach her about the unconventional situation that she was going to be part of. It would have been so much more preferable if Debbie could have given her daughter a warm, loving, conventional family. She would have to work extra hard at smoothing the path ahead for both of them.

'What time is Marcel coming?' Emma asked as mother and daughter sat at the kitchen table.

'He's going to try and get here as soon as he can leave the hospital,' Debbie said, hoping it would be sooner rather than later. Since she'd told Emma that Marcel was going to come to the house that evening, she'd been full of impatience to see him. Debbie found more and more that she was glad she wasn't going to be alone when she gave Emma the news about the baby.

She spooned some pasta on to Emma's plate before adding some tuna.

Emma began eating hungrily before pausing. 'Aren't you going to have some, Mummy?'

'I'm not hungry yet, darling. I'll have something later.'

'Will Marcel be staying for supper?'

'He might be. It depends on whether he has to go back to the hospital or not.'

But most importantly, she thought, it depends on how things go between us after we've announced the news to you!

Emma finished everything on her plate before putting down her fork and taking a drink of milk. Halfway through the glass she stopped, pricking up her ears as she heard the sound of tyres crunching on the drive.

'That's Marcel. I recognise the sound of his car.' Putting down her glass, she jumped down from the table and ran out into the hall, yanking open the front door and shrieking with delight.

Debbie waited in the kitchen, trying to calm her nerves. She could hear her daughter's excited voice mingling with Marcel's deep tones.

Emma arrived back first. 'Look at the flowers Marcel has brought you, Mummy! Aren't they beautiful?'

Emma was completely dwarfed by the huge bouquet of roses she was carrying. 'Can I get that big vase to put them in? I'll be very careful and I won't break the stems like I did last time you let me do the flowers.'

'I'll help you,' Debbie said quietly, as she reached for the huge earthenware vase before placing it on the table.

She looked across at Marcel who was still standing in the doorway of the kitchen as if he was uncertain of his welcome. She smiled to reassure him.

'Thank you so much, Marcel,' she said. 'I love roses.'

'I know.'

'Would you like a drink?'

'Later perhaps. Shall we talk first?'

She nodded. 'I'll just help Emma with the roses and then— Ooh, careful, darling…'

Debbie reached out to catch hold of the huge vase before it toppled off the table. 'I'll put the water in and then you can help to arrange them.'

'Let me snip off the ends of the roses, Emma,' Marcel said. 'Where do you keep your scissors?'

Emma pulled open the cutlery drawer and held the scissors towards Marcel, taking great care to hold them with the handles toward him.

'I can see you've been well trained how to handle instruments,' Marcel said as he took the scissors from Emma and began to snip at the stalks of the roses.

'Oh, yes. My mummy taught me how to handle knives and scissors. My French grandpa used to be a surgeon and my English grandmother was a surgeon as well. Like you are, Marcel. Did you know that?'

'Yes, your mummy told me.' Marcel said as he continued snipping.

Emma climbed up on a chair to watch, solemnly handing over each rose in turn. 'Grandma died before I was born but I've seen pictures of her. She was very beautiful. A bit like Mummy really, only with blonde hair. That's where my blonde hair came from. Mummy got her dark hair from Grandpa André.'

Emma watched Marcel closely. 'You're very clever at cutting, aren't you? Do you have to cut people open and then sew them up again?'

'Sometimes,' Marcel said solemnly. 'Not as much as I used to now that I work in Accident and Emergency.'

'I can't decide whether to be a surgeon or work in Accident and Emergency when I grow up. What do you think I should do, Marcel?'

'Well, you could do both. You could go through all your surgical training, work for a while as a surgeon and then go into Accident and Emergency, like I did. Everything's possible once you've finished all your training.'

He paused. 'I might go back to being a surgeon one day. Who knows what will happen in the future?'

He looked across at Debbie, his eyes giving nothing away. As their eyes met she felt a tremor of apprehension. It was so good to be here with Marcel behaving like a real father, as if he were part of the family. But for how long could she hope for this kind of cosy intimacy?

Emma began helping Debbie to arrange the prepared roses, taking great care as she put each one separately into the vase.

'Why did you change from being a surgeon?' Emma asked.

Marcel put the final rose into the vase. 'That's a long story. I'll tell you one day. But now I think Mummy has got something to tell you.'

Debbie picked up the vase and placed it on the kitchen dresser. 'Shall we all sit round the table?'

Emma looked at her quizzically. 'Is it an important something you're going to tell me? You look kind of…fierce. I haven't done something wrong, have I?'

Debbie smiled as she tried to adopt a more relaxed appearance. Years from now, Emma would remember the evening when the grown-ups explained how she would have a baby brother.

'No, you haven't done anything wrong, darling. Come and sit here next to me. I've got something really exciting to tell you…'

'Is Grandpa André coming to see us?'

'No, it's even more exciting.' She took a deep breath as her eyes locked with Marcel's across the table. 'I'm going to have a baby.'

Emma's eyes widened. 'Honestly? Mummy, that's wonderful!' She flung her arms around Debbie's neck, kissing her cheek enthusiastically. 'Oh, thank you! I knew you could get a baby if—'

She broke off and sat down on her chair, looking perplexed. 'But you can't be having a baby. You haven't got a daddy to help you, have you? Unless…'

She looked across the table at Marcel. 'Did you plant a baby seed in Mummy's tummy?'

Marcel nodded solemnly. 'Yes, I'm the baby's daddy.'

Emma digested this piece of information but still looked puzzled. 'I'm not sure I understand.'

'Marcel will be the new baby's daddy but not your daddy,' Debbie said.

Emma considered this for a few seconds. 'But he could be my second daddy, couldn't he?'

Marcel smiled with relief. 'I'd love to be your second daddy.'

Debbie swallowed the lump in her throat as she watched the two people she loved most in the world bonding.

'But, Mummy…' Emma turned to fix her puzzled eyes on Debbie. 'You said that when the daddy puts the seed in the mummy, they have to love each other so they can have a special cuddle. Does that mean that you love Marcel?'

Debbie looked across the table at Marcel. She could feel tears pricking behind her eyelids. She mustn't cry, but the situation was all too poignant. She would love to say that, yes, she loved Marcel, but…

As her eyes met Marcel's she saw an expression of deep tenderness. He stood up and came round the table to put an arm around her shoulders.

'I don't know whether Debbie loves me, but I certainly love her,' he said, his voice husky with emotion.

Debbie was still holding back the tears but now they were tears of happiness. She could feel Marcel's arm around her shoulders, so comforting, so reassuring. She couldn't believe he'd said he loved her.

'That's OK, then,' Emma said. 'Marcel planted the baby seed because he loves you, Mummy. Do you love him?'

'Yes, I do,' she whispered hoarsely.

She could feel his arm tighten on her shoulders.

He leaned down so that he could speak quietly to her.

'Does that mean we can negotiate new terms in our contract?'

She smiled. 'I think we'd better.'

'What does negotiate mean, Marcel?'

Marcel sat down on a chair and hoisted Emma onto his lap. 'It's what people do when they get together and talk over something that's a problem. Your mother and I had a problem but I think we've just solved it.'

'Oh, good! You don't need me to help you, do you? The teacher sets us problems at school and I'm quite good at getting them right.'

'It's kind of you to offer, Emma,' Marcel said gently, 'but I think your mummy and I can work this one out by ourselves.'

He reached across and took hold of Debbie's hand.

It was only a squeeze of his fingers but to Debbie it was a magic moment she would never forget.

Later, much later, when Emma was fast asleep, Debbie and Marcel sat on the sitting-room sofa, their hands locked together.

'I didn't dare to hope you'd changed,' Marcel said. 'You were so intent on remaining independent. And I thought you'd been hurt so badly before that you'd never be able to love again.'

'I tried so hard not to love you. But I couldn't help falling in love. And then I just kept on pretending nothing had changed because I thought you wanted to stick to our original plan. I thought that if I made my true feelings clear, I would frighten you away and we wouldn't even be friends.'

'I very soon realised that I wanted to be more than a part-time father. I wanted to be with you all the time.

But you were so unpredictable. Especially the last few weeks. I tried to put that down to your pregnancy but—'

'It was because I had a long conversation on the phone with my father. He told me that it had been very hard for him to keep up the pretence that all was well when I was a child. He'd always been in love with my mother. He wanted to marry her but she refused him. All his life while he was giving me so much love he suffered because his love for my mother was unrequited. When I told him about our baby plan and explained I'd fallen in love with you, he advised me to cool our relationship. He said he didn't want me to suffer as he had done.'

Marcel drew her against him. 'I'll never do anything to make you suffer, Debbie,' he whispered.

She snuggled against him. It felt so wonderful to be so sure that he loved her. She eased herself out of his arms and looked up at him.

'Thank you for letting me go it alone for the first three months of my pregnancy. Now that I know how you really feel about me, I'd like you to be in on every stage I go through.'

He smiled. 'That's a relief! I haven't felt like a real father until today.' He hesitated. 'Actually, I've set the wheels in motion to find a replacement for your maternity leave.'

She gave him a wry smile. 'That was one area we didn't agree on, wasn't it?'

'All we've got to agree on is when you stop working. The medical agency I've been dealing with in London has chosen the ideal candidate. She's working in Accident and Emergency in a hospital in the north of England but has agreed to spend a year working here at St Martin.'

'A year!'

Marcel grinned. 'I'm covering all eventualities. You might want to spend a few months at home with the baby. She can work alongside you if you do choose to come back soon after the birth. I've got to let her have the date she'll be required to start so that she can give in her notice.'

'I see. She's a doctor in A and E at the moment, you say?'

'Yes, her name's Jacqueline Manson. Likes to be called Jacky, I believe. She's got a French mother and an English father so she's totally bilingual, which will be useful. The question I need you to answer is when will you agree to give up work?'

'I know you suggested three months before due date, but how about two months?'

'OK. We could agree to compromise. I'll ensure that Dr Manson is here three months before.' He hurried on before Debbie could intervene. 'That way, she'll be there if you do decide to stop earlier. And if you actually do continue till two months before, you can help Jacky to settle into her new job and also she can take over from you any time you might be feeling tired.'

Debbie smiled and held her hand out. 'A good compromise. Let's shake on that. Now, is that the end of the negotiations?'

'There's one more question I have to ask you,' he said, his tone changing to one of deep tenderness.

She looked up into his eyes and a tremor of excitement ran through her.

'Darling, will you marry me?' he asked, his voice vibrant with emotion.

'Yes,' she whispered, her heart so full of love she could barely speak.

He lowered his head and kissed her gently on the mouth. She parted her lips to savour the wonderful moment. The moment when she knew that all her seemingly impossible dreams were coming true.

'I don't want to tire you,' he whispered. 'But it would be wonderful to cement our new agreement in the appropriate manner.'

'I'm not in the least bit tired…now.' She held out her arms towards him. 'If you were to help me negotiate the stairs…'

The ancient church of St Martin was completely full. Some people were standing at the back of the church, others had congregated in the churchyard. There was a brisk wind coming off the sea. Just five days to Christmas the weather was predictably chilly.

As Debbie walked up the path on her father's arm, she looked up at the sky. A few clouds floated overhead but no snow—yet. The odds of a white Christmas were shortening every day. For a moment she allowed herself to imagine how wonderful it would be to be marooned inside by the log fire on Christmas Day with Marcel and Emma, watching the snow drifting down outside the windows.

'You make a beautiful bride,' her father said quietly. 'I'm so glad everything's worked out for you. You're a very lucky girl.'

'I know,' Debbie said. 'I still can't believe that I'm living my perfect dream.'

She felt a little tug on the back of her white satin dress. Emma, looking like a little angel in her long fairy-tale bridesmaid's dress, was saying something in a loud stage whisper.

'Mummy, I just trod on my skirt and a bit of it got torn. Can you sew it up for me?'

The people standing on the edge of the path were admiring the feisty little bridesmaid who was in no way overawed by the occasion. Debbie smiled as she bent down to speak to her daughter.

'I'll mend your dress when we get home, darling. Oh, it doesn't look too bad. But you'll have to hold your skirt up so you don't trip.'

Jacky Manson, the new doctor who would be replacing Debbie at the hospital, stepped forward. 'I've got a couple of safety pins in my bag, Emma. Let me fix it for you. It won't take a moment.'

'Thanks, Jacky,' Debbie said, as her new friend bent down to pin Emma's dress up.

Debbie had become very fond of the new English doctor who she had been liaising with in the lead up to her taking her place while she was on maternity leave. But she was something of a mystery. Debbie wondered why a first-class doctor like Jacky, with an excellent job in England, would want to spend a year filling in for someone on maternity leave. It was her considered opinion that there was a man involved in Jacky's decision.

'You make a beautiful bridesmaid, Emma,' Jacky said as she hid the pins at the back of the torn dress. As she stepped back to the edge of the path she whispered, 'Good luck, Debbie!'

'Thank you.'

'Thanks, Jacky,' Emma said. 'Mummy, which home are we going back to? Can we go to Marcel's home?'

'Yes, we're going to live there all the time soon. That will be our home.'

'Ooh, lovely!'

André touched his daughter's arm. 'They're waiting for us in the church, *chérie.*'

'I'm ready, Papa,' Debbie said, taking his arm again. As she moved forward she could feel the rustle of the petticoat under her satin gown. Marcel had insisted on taking her to Paris to choose her wedding dress. She'd enlisted the help of Louise and had chosen a very simple beautifully cut gown at one of the designer boutiques her stepmother frequented.

Marcel had spent the morning with André as both men had been forbidden to see the gown until the wedding day. It had been a relief to find that the two most important men in her life got on together as if they were old friends. André had completely forgotten his misgivings about his future son-in-law now that he realised the situation was completely different to his own.

Despite her pregnancy, her shape had changed very little. The gown was her usual size but the seamstress in the boutique had let out a couple of seams at the waist. The sleeves were long and fitted closely to her arms. At the wrist of each sleeve was a strip of white faux mink, which helped to keep out the cold. A wider strip of the same faux fur adorned the hem of her fluted, exquisitely embroidered gown.

As she walked into the church she felt as if she was a princess going to meet her prince. The haunting music hung in the air as she went down the aisle. He was standing in front of the altar, her handsome prince. Her heart gave a little leap of excitement as he turned to look at her. His expression was one of love and admiration as she left her father's side to join him. The music ceased but her dream continued.

Looking up into Marcel's eyes, Debbie knew she would come down to earth one day soon. And there would be times ahead when they might have to face difficult problems. But the most important thing that would help them through any problem was knowing that they both loved each other.

And love changed everything…

EPILOGUE

DEBBIE put baby Thiery back in his cot on her side of the bed. She lingered a while, her fingers gently caressing the soft downy hair on his tiny head. The hair was still baby blond but it would probably change. He had long legs already like Marcel. And she could tell already that he was going to be handsome just like his father.

Marcel stirred in his sleep and opened his eyes.

'Did you just feed Thiery?'

Debbie smiled. 'Yes, and you slept through it. You didn't hear him crying out at the beginning when I changed his nappy?'

Marcel raised himself on one elbow so that he could look down at his beautiful wife.

'I didn't hear a thing.'

'That's what you always say!'

'Well, I'd be no good at breastfeeding, would I? For a six-week-old baby, Thiery is a hungry little man. Would you like me to bring you something to drink, hot, cold from the fridge or…?'

'No, thanks, I'm working my way through this flask of water to replace the fluids I'm giving out.'

'You know, motherhood suits you.' He leaned forward and caressed her cheek lovingly. You always look so radiant now…even in the middle of the night.'

'I'm happy, that's the reason. I've got everything I ever wanted. Emma's happy as well. Have you noticed?'

Marcel nodded. 'She adores her little brother. She told me today she didn't mind he was a boy, but next time could we try for a sister for her.'

Debbie laughed. 'Did you explain that we don't get a choice in the matter?'

'No, I changed the subject quickly. I thought we could deal with that one together some time.'

'And the fact that mummies like to have a breathing space between babies,' Debbie said.

'But not too much of a space,' Marcel said.

She smiled. 'Of course not. When I had my six-week check-up today I was declared completely fit. Everything's back in place.' She hesitated. 'So all the signs are that we could make the space between Thiery and the next baby quite small.'

Marcel kissed the side of her cheek. 'You're wonderful! So you've really decided not to go back to work for a while? I'm so glad!'

'I think Jacky will be, too. She's enjoying her work at the hospital. I was right about her, wasn't I?'

'Oh, you mean about a man being involved with her decision to come over to France? Yes, you were, but it's all a bit complicated, isn't it? I wouldn't like to speculate how…'

'Well, I think it's terribly romantic!'

'And you love a good romance, don't you?'

'Of course I do. Especially ours. I think our life here is so romantic. Listen, can you hear the waves out there?'

Marcel nodded. He drew her into his arms.

'And can you smell the scent of the roses in the garden?'

He nuzzled his lips against her hair. 'Yes, I can.'

'Marcel, let's go and walk in the garden for a few

minutes. It's still warm out there. I want to walk with my bare feet on the grass and look at the moon. We'll leave the windows wide open so we can hear if Thiery cries…'

'Sounds good to me.'

She held out her hand towards him. 'And when we come back, now that I've been given a clean bill of health, will you hold me close and…?'

Marcel gave her a rakish grin. 'You mean we could have one of those special cuddles that mummies and daddies have when they want to make a baby?'

Debbie laughed. 'That's exactly what I mean!'

Marcel took hold of her hand and brought it to his lips. He knew he would always love his beautiful, fascinating wife. She seemed to make everyday situations into an adventure. It was early days in the big adventure of their marriage, but each day seemed to be better than the one that had gone before…

MILLS & BOON®

Live the emotion

_Medical
romance™

THE HEART SURGEON'S PROPOSAL
by *Meredith Webber* *(Jimmie's Children's Unit)*

Paediatric anaesthetist Maggie Walsh fell in love with surgery fellow Phil Park when they both joined the elite Children's Cardiac Unit. But he never seemed to look her way – until the night they fell into bed! Now Maggie is pregnant! Phil will do the right thing – for the baby's sake – but Maggie won't consent to a loveless marriage...

EMERGENCY AT THE ROYAL by *Joanna Neil*

Dr Katie Sherbourn knows she shouldn't get too close to A&E consultant Drew Bradley. It would upset her ill father and alienate her from her beloved family. But memories of her relationship with Drew leave Katie yearning for his touch. And working closely with him at the Royal forces her to confront her feelings...

THE MEDICINE MAN by *Dianne Drake* (24/7)

Chayton Ducheneaux turned his back on his Sioux roots for life as a high-powered Chicago surgeon. He'd never give it up to return home. But then he meets the reservation doctor, Joanna Killian. She's dedicated, determined – and beautiful. And as the attraction between them grows Chay learns what being a doctor – and a man – is really about...

On sale 3rd June 2005

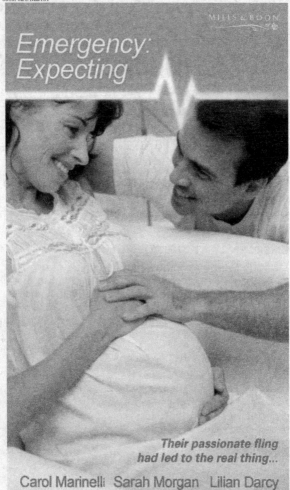

FREE

4 BOOKS AND A SURPRISE GIFT!

We would like to take this opportunity to thank you for reading this Mills & Boon® book by offering you the chance to take FOUR more specially selected titles from the Medical Romance™ series absolutely FREE! We're also making this offer to introduce you to the benefits of the Reader Service™—

- ★ **FREE home delivery**
- ★ **FREE gifts and competitions**
- ★ **FREE monthly Newsletter**
- ★ **Books available before they're in the shops**
- ★ **Exclusive Reader Service offers**

Accepting these FREE books and gift places you under no obligation to buy; you may cancel at any time, even after receiving your free shipment. Simply complete your details below and return the entire page to the address below. You don't even need a stamp!

YES! Please send me 4 free Medical Romance books and a surprise gift. I understand that unless you hear from me, I will receive 6 superb new titles every month for just £2.75 each, postage and packing free. I am under no obligation to purchase any books and may cancel my subscription at any time. The free books and gift will be mine to keep in any case.

M5ZEE

Ms/Mrs/Miss/Mr.................................Initials ....
BLOCK CAPITALS PLEASE

Surname ....

Address ....

....

....Postcode ....

Send this whole page to:

The Reader Service, FREEPOST CN81, Croydon, CR9 3WZ

Offer valid in UK only and is not available to current Reader Service™subscribers to this series. Overseas and Eire please write for details. We reserve the right to refuse an application and applicants must be aged 18 years or over. Only one application per household. Terms and prices subject to change without notice. Offer expires 31st August 2005. As a result of this application, you may receive offers from Harlequin Mills & Boon and other carefully selected companies. If you would prefer not to share in this opportunity please write to The Data Manager at PO Box 676, Richmond, TW9 1WU.

Mills & Boon® is a registered trademark owned by Harlequin Mills & Boon Limited.
Medical Romance™ is being used as a trademark. The Reader Service™ is being used as a trademark.